Taxi

Aflame Books
2 The Green
Laverstock
Wiltshire
SP1 1QS
United Kingdom
email: info@aflamebooks.com

ISBN: 9781906300029
First published in 2008 by Aflame Books

First published in Arabic as *Taxi,* by Dar El Shorouk, Cairo, 2007.

Cover design by the author. Cover images: Details of
'Dahroug coffee' (oil on wood 100cmx70cm) and
'Country House' (oil on canvas 100cmx70cm)
both by Nabil Lahoud.
Cover photo of Cairo taxi 56 taken by the author

Printed in Poland
www.polskabook.pl

Khaled Al Khamissi

Translated by Jonathan Wright

I dedicate this book

To the life which is latent in the words of simple people
May it swallow the void which has haunted us for many years

Our Lady, with the infant Jesus in her arms, came down to earth to visit a monastery. In their joy, the monks stood in line to pay their respects: one of them recited poetry, another showed her illuminated images from the Bible, another recited the names of all of the saints. At the end of the line was a humble monk who had never had the chance to learn from the wise men of his time. His parents were simple people who worked in a traveling circus. When his turn came, the monks wanted to end the payment of respects, fearful that he would embarass them. But he too wanted to show his love for the Virgin. Embarrassed, and sensing the disapproval of the brothers, he took some oranges from his pocket and began to toss them in the air – juggling as his parents in the circus had taught him. It was only then that the infant Jesus smiled and clapped his hands with joy. And it was only to the humble monk that the Virgin held out her arms, allowing him to hold her son for a while.

Paulo Coelho in *Maktub*

Words that need to be said

For years I've been a prize customer for taxis, taking them through all the highways and byways of Cairo, so much so that I know the lanes and the potholes better than any driver. (A little conceit never did any harm).

I'm one of those people who likes to talk to taxi drivers, for they really are one of the barometers of the unruly Egyptian street. This book contains between its covers some of the stories I shared with taxi drivers and some of the things that happened while I was in their company between April 2005 and March 2006.

I say that the book contains some of the stories and not all of them because lawyer friends of mine told me that publishing them all would guarantee my being thrown in jail on libel charges and that it could be dangerous to record the precise names in jokes or particular stories which are widely circulated on the streets of Egypt. Dangerous, young man. That's a pity because those popular stories and jokes will be lost unless recorded.

I have tried to relate these stories as they are, in the language of the street – a special, blunt, vital and honest language quite different from the language of salons and seminars that we are used to.

My role here is certainly not to check the accuracy of the information I collected and wrote down. What matters here is what a particular individual says in society at a particular moment of history on a certain subject because sociology transcends the factual in the scale of priorities of this book.

Taxi drivers belong mostly to an economically deprived sector of the population. They work at a trade which is physically exhausting: sitting constantly in dilapidated cars wrecks their spines and the ceaseless shouting that goes on in the streets of Cairo destroys their nervous systems. The endless heavy traffic drains them psychologically and the struggle to make a living, a literal struggle, strains the sinews of their bodies to the limit. Add to that the constant arguing back and forth with passengers, in the absence of any system for calculating fares, and with the police who generally treat them in a way that would make the Marquis de Sade feel comfortable in his grave.

On top of that the income from a taxi, if calculated scientifically, that is taking into account all the elements such as depreciation, the driver's wages, taxes and the cost of spare parts and of fines and so on, we'll find that it's 100 per cent a losing proposition. The drivers think the taxi is making money because they don't allow for many of the unseen costs. So most of the taxis are falling to pieces, miserable and dirty, and the drivers work on them like slaves.

A number of decrees have encouraged an unprecedented interest in the taxi business, to the extent that the number of taxis in Greater Cairo has risen to 80,000. The most important decree, issued in the second half of the 90s, was to allow any old car to be converted into a taxi. The second decree brought banks into the business of giving car loans, which included loans for taxis. In that way a large number of unemployed people joined the ranks of the taxi drivers and began a really tortuous path to cover the instalments on their loans. The effort of these tortured wretches has been transformed into more profit for the banks, the car companies and the importers of spare parts.

As a result, you now find taxi drivers from all walks of life and of all levels of education, starting with illiterates up to people with master's degrees, although I have not yet met taxi drivers with doctorates.

These taxi drivers have a broad knowledge of society because in practice they live on the streets and they meet an amazing mix of people every day. Through the conversations they hold they reflect an amalgam of points of view which are most representative of the poor in Egyptian society.

It must be said that often I see in the political analysis of some drivers a greater depth than I find among a number of political analysts who pontificate far and wide. For the culture of this nation comes to light through the simple people, and the Egyptian people really are a teacher to anyone who wishes to learn.

Khaled Al Khamissi
Cairo, March 2006

Taxi

One

My God, how old is this driver? And how old is this car? I couldn't believe my eyes when I sat down next to him. The wrinkles in his face were as many as the stars in the sky, and every wrinkle pressed gently against the next, to make the kind of Egyptian face created by the sculptor Mahmoud Mukhtar. His hands gripped the steering wheel, and as he stretched out or retracted his arms, I noticed the prominent veins, like watercourses nourishing dry land with Nile water. He trembled slightly but the steering wheel did not move to the left or right. The car kept moving dead ahead, and from his eyes, beneath his giant eyelids, there emanated a state of inner peace, pervading me and the world with a sense of reassurance.

Just by sitting at his side, through the force field he emitted, I felt that life was good. For some reason I remembered my favourite Belgian poet, Jacques Brel, and how wrong he was when he suggested that any form of death was preferable to growing old. If Brel had sat next to this man, he would have rubbed that poem out.

"You must have been driving a long time," I said.

"I've been driving a taxi since 1948," the driver replied.

I hadn't imagined that he had been in the trade for close to 60 years. I didn't dare ask how old he was but I found myself asking about the outcome. "And what, I wonder, is the essence of your experience, that you can tell to someone like me so that I can learn from it?" I said.

"A black ant on a black rock on a pitch-black night, provided for by God," he answered.

"What do you mean?" I asked.

"I'll tell you a story about something that happened to me this month so that you understand what I mean."

"Please do."

"I fell seriously ill for 10 days and I couldn't move from bed. Of course I'm pretty poor and live from hand to mouth. After a week there wasn't a penny in the house. I knew, but my wife was trying to hide it from me. So I say to her: 'What are we going to do, missus?' 'Everything's just fine, Abu Hussein,' she answers, though she'd been begging food from all the neighbours. Of course my children have enough worries of their own, one having married off half his kids and not knowing how to marry off the others, another having a sick grandchild and running around the hospitals with him, I mean there's no point asking them for anything. It should be me helping them. After ten days I said to the old woman: 'I've got to go out to work.' She insisted I stay and kept yelling that if I went out it would be the death of me. To tell the truth, I wasn't up to going out but I told myself I had to. I told her a white lie and said I would sit at the coffee shop for an hour, for a change of air because I was going to suffocate. I went out and started the car and said: 'Oh God, oh Provider.' I drove along until I reached the Orman Gardens and came across a Peugeot 504 broken down and its driver waving at me. I stopped and he came up to me and said he had an Arab man going to the airport and could I take him because his car had broken down? Do you notice the wisdom of God? He had a Peugeot 504 in prime condition and it broke down! I told him I'd take him.

"The passenger got in with me and he turned out to be from

Oman, from Sultan Qaboos's place. He asked me how much I would charge and I told him whatever you pay. He double checked that whatever he paid I would take, and I told him okay.

"On the way I found out that he was going to the freight depot because he had some goods to clear. I told him that my grandson worked there and could help him with the customs clearance. He said okay, and in fact I went and found my grandson there and on duty. Take note here that, of course, I might not have found him. We cleared the things he wanted to clear and I took him back to Dokki.

"Again he asked me: 'What will you charge, old man?'

"I said we'd agreed on whatever he would pay, and he went and gave me 50 pounds, which I took and thanked him and started the car. He asked me: 'Satisfied?' and I answered that I was.

"Then he told me: 'Look, old man, the customs duty should have been 1,400 pounds and I paid 600 pounds. That makes a difference of 800 pounds that I've saved myself and that means it's your due, plus 200 pounds as the taxi fare. Here's 1,000 pounds and the 50 you have is a gift from me.'

"See, that means one fare brought me 1,000 pounds. I could work a month and not earn that. See, God brought me out of the house and made the Peugeot 504 break down and set up all the elements for Him to provide me with this money. Because it's not your earnings and the money's not yours. It's all God's. That's the only thing I have learnt in my life."

I got out of the taxi regretfully, for I had hoped to sit with him for hours and hours more. But unfortunately I too had an appointment, part of the same constant struggle to make a living.

Two

Two

I got into a taxi on Arab League Street in front of the Zamalek Club wall and the driver's face was flushed bright red as though he was about to explode. I really felt that a snake had found its way into his arteries and was writhing within from excessive anger, or that he had just had a blood clot in the brain.

"Never you mind, it will all pass," I told him.

"Beg your pardon, something wrong, sir?" he replied.

"You looked annoyed, so I thought I'd tell you not to worry."

"I'm not annoyed, I'm going to die," said the driver.

"But what's the matter? There's nothing in the world worth all that."

"Oh yes there is," said the driver. "I work my butt off to feed the kids and some bastard comes along and takes it from me. Then you tell me whether it's worth it or not? Yes, it's worth it. I'm worked to exhaustion, not like you, sir, all calm and serene."

"What are you talking about?" I asked. "You want to take out your anger on me! Just tell me what happened."

"I picked up a guy in Nasr City and he told me to go to Muhandiseen, and I said okay. The road was jammed and the flyover was completely blocked. I thought he wouldn't take that into account when paying the fare but no problem, because it was me that didn't fix a price with him in advance. When I came down on to the Agouza corniche, he told me to turn into Sphinx Square and I did. He said: 'Take the first turning and park here past Omar Effendi because we're going to set up a checkpoint here.'

"Checkpoint! What a disaster, I said to myself. Anyway, he turned out to be a police sergeant in plain clothes and obviously he wasn't going to pay me anything. I stopped the cab and the next thing is he's saying: 'Your licence and your papers, you son of a bitch.' 'But why, officer?' I said. 'I haven't done anything.' 'Your licences,' he said and I pulled out five pounds. 'That's no use,' he said, so I pulled out ten pounds. 'That's no use,' he said. Anyway, he took 20 pounds and the bastard got out. By God, and I trust you'll believe me, that's all I had earned today since I filled up with petrol. I could readily have throttled him but I thought of my kids and the old woman. But I'm an idiot, because now I'll die from the bitterness. I should have killed him, a life for a life."

"He was just like a thug, frankly," I said.

"Thuggery, big time," said the driver. "There's not one of those bastards who doesn't take bribes or steal.* May God destroy their father's house just as every day they destroy ours."

One of the most popular pastimes for Cairo taxi drivers is insulting the Interior Ministry, and respecting, revering and venerating it at the same time, because they – the drivers and the Interior Ministry's traffic department – are always out on the streets. Stories in this area abound, but this story was a violent slap in the face.

I had often heard condemnation of the policemen in my magic Cairo but I had never been as sympathetic as I was with this poor man, the victim of this policeman.

---

* Author's note: Some people advised me to write that some of them take bribes, rather than all of them, as the driver said, but I didn't take their advice because he was absolutely in no state to talk reasonably or refrain from some exaggeration.

The new concept of policemen with the title of *amin* was a beautiful dream in the early 1970s, an *amin* on the streets in his beautiful uniform, walking along so elegant, proud as a peacock, and which of us does not remember the words of Salah Jahin in the film *Watch out for Zouzou*, when he likens the *amin* Ismallah to a diplomat?

How did this dream, over the past 30 years, turn into a nightmare haunting the streets of Egypt?

Three

Three

One of the direct social effects of the Kefaya opposition movement on the streets of Cairo is that it pushed up the taxi meters on demonstration days. Of course by meters I mean the taxi fares because the meter is there just as an ornament to embellish the car and to tear the trousers of customers who sit next to the driver.

On that particular day I was in Shooting Club Street in Dokki and heading downtown, standing looking for a taxi. Whenever I waved to one and shouted out: "Downtown", the driver would brush me off and keep on driving. That was strange. It took me back to the days of the 1980s when finding Ali Baba's treasure was easier than finding an empty taxi. You only have to look back at the cartoons of that period to see how taxi customers like me suffered from the 'yellow towel' folded over the meter. Please God don't bring such days back! Now you stand out for less than a minute to ride a beautiful taxi and you can choose from among dozens of vehicles, except that day, until one driver obliged, stopped and asked seven pounds for the trip. "Why?" I shouted.

"There are demonstrations and the world's turned upside down and it'll take me an hour to get you there," he answered.

"I tell you, seven pounds won't be enough. I'll do it for ten pounds." To cut a long story short, I agreed to pay ten pounds for the trip, for which I usually pay three pounds.

It was indeed impossible to move. The cars were bumper to bumper and on top of each other on the street, moving not an inch, as though we were imprisoned in a giant garage.

"What's up?" I asked

"Demonstrations," said the driver. "Dunno why. There are about 200 people holding banners and around them about 2,000 riot police and 200 officers, and riot police trucks blocking everything."

"All this crowd for 200 people?" I said.

"The crowd's not from the demonstration, and it's not much of a demonstration in the first place. In the old days we used to go out on the streets with 50,000 people, with 100,000. But now there's nothing that matters. How many people are going to step out of their front door for something no one understands? And the government's terrified, its knees are shaking. I mean, one puff and the government will fall, a government without knees." He laughed out loud.

"You think the government needs legs?" I said.

"Nothing doing with the government, puffed up with false pride. But the problem's with us," said the driver.

"How so?" I said.

"You know what was the beginning of the end?"

"What?"

"The 18th and 19th of January," he said.

I was stunned by this answer, which I was hearing for the first time. I had expected many conventional responses, but the 18th and 19th of January! This was new, and I wondered whether the driver knew that the demonstrations on those days, which President Sadat called 'The Uprising of the Thieves', took place in 1977. I don't know for certain why this stupid question came to my mind but I put it to him anyway. "What year was that?" I said.

"In the 70s, I mean about 1979," he said.

"And why was that the beginning of the end?"

"Those were the last serious demonstrations on the streets. In the 1960s we did many protests and in the 1970s before the 1973 war they were very frequent. After that Sadat, God curse him wherever he goes, issued decrees that put up the price of everything. The world turned upside down. People understood politics and they went out on the streets and made Sadat go back on his word. At the time we heard he'd taken fright and fled to Aswan and was saying that if he was overthrown properly, he'd flee to Sudan, the coward. My God, anyone could have seized power that day, but there wasn't anyone, just a bunch of wretches wanting prices to come down.

"In Abdel Nasser's time we went on demonstrations that made a real impact and suddenly we would find him there among us in Tahrir Square. He hadn't gone off to Aswan or even gone home. That's what happened after the Defeat, can't remember exactly when."

"I still haven't understood why the 18th and 19th of January were the beginning of the end," I interjected.

"After that the government realised that it had to get its act together, and that these demonstrations had become a serious danger to them. The 18th and 19th of January were not just anything, that was the start of a revolution, but you know what, it wasn't completed. And since then the government has planted in us a fear of hunger. It's made every woman hold her husband by the arm and say to him: 'Mind you don't go out. The kids will die.' They planted hunger in the belly of every Egyptian, a terror that made everyone look out for himself or say 'Why should I make it my problem?', so that's why the 18th and 19th of January were the beginning of the end."

Were the 18th and 19th of January really the beginning of the end? And what is this end that the driver was talking about with such simplicity and such certainty?

Four

I came out of the Cinema Galaxy after watching Yusry Nasrallah's excellent film *Bab el Chams*. I'd seen the two parts one after the other and I was in a state of ecstasy and extreme elation at this stunning work. My heart was pounding and I felt I was walking two inches off the ground.

I stopped a taxi in Manyal Street and before sitting down I asked the driver to take me downtown. "Right you are," he answered faintly.

I got in, shut the door, looked in front of me and saw the cave scene from *Bab el Chams* on the windscreen of the taxi, the only space that wasn't taken up, and my heart filled with the beautiful music of Tamer Karawan. Then, after a while, I realised that the car wasn't moving and the road in front of us was empty.

I looked at the driver and found him in a deep slumber. I didn't know what to do. Should I get out and leave him to sleep? I hesitated a while and in the end I touched his shoulder. He shuddered in alarm, then robotically put his hand on the gear lever and set the car in motion. "Where do you want to go?" he asked. "Downtown," I said. He apologised for his lapse but within a few seconds the car was veering off towards the left.

I looked at the driver and found his whole body was also veering to the left, and he was again fast asleep.

I shouted in alarm and grabbed the wheel. The driver woke up, saved the situation and again apologised. I asked him to stop so that I could get out. He swore blind that he wouldn't fall asleep again and that he would deliver me downtown safe and sound.

My elation from Yusry's film had vanished and my heart had stopped fluttering. Instead a sense of anxiety and foreboding had gripped me, and indeed, before a minute had passed, I found the car veering to the left again and the driver's body was leaning right towards me until his shoulder touched mine.

I shouted out again and he straightened the wheel again, assuring me hurriedly that he wasn't asleep. Then he started talking to keep himself awake. "You see, I've been driving this taxi for three days now without a break," he said.

"Three days? How do you manage that?"

"Today's the 27th," he said. "I've got three days left before I have to pay the installment on the car. The installment's 1,200 pounds a month. Three days ago I gave my wife a solemn oath that I wouldn't come home without paying the whole installment. I only had 200 pounds towards it then and I haven't left the car since the time I got in, except to piss, excuse my language. I eat in the car and drink in the car but I don't sleep. I have to get the money and I have to pay it by the end of the month."

"But what use is it if you get the money for the installment and die?" I asked. "Because you could have an accident and end up dead, and take me with you too."

"The rogue has nine lives, and our lives are in the hands of God," he answered. "And yours truly is a real rogue. I'm nearly there, just some three days to go and I'll have made the money for the installment."

"Okay, so why don't you go and have yourself two or three

hours' sleep? It won't make any difference. Make it three days and three hours, man."

"I swore a solemn oath, and you don't understand, sir. We live from day to day and meal to meal. I mean, if I went home I'd find a hundred and one disasters. I'd find the children hadn't eaten and their mother at her wit's end. No sir, no way! I won't get out of this taxi till I reach Ibrahim Issa and pay him the installment and it's all wrapped up. After that I'll go home."

Deeply troubled, I left him. After I got out of the taxi, I stood and looked after the car as it drove off into the distance, expecting at any moment that the driver would fall asleep and disaster would strike. But the car did not swerve as it drove off and disappeared completely from my field of vision.

Five

"People wonder why the economy's screwed up," the driver said. "It's screwed up because of people. Would you believe it, a country like Egypt, the people here spend more than 20 billion pounds a year on telephone calls. Twenty billion pounds, I mean, if we didn't talk for two or three years, would Egypt be any different?

"The people are crazy, by God. People have nothing to eat and everyone's walking around with a mobile and a cigarette in his mouth.

"Men who should have brains and they spend all their money on these two disasters – telephones and cigarettes. And in the end they say it's because the state of the country isn't as it should be.

"Everyone's money goes into the pocket of four companies — Telecom Egypt, Mobinil, Vodafone and Eastern Tobacco.* And the advertisements, God damn them, keep putting

---

* Author's note: Egypt has one of the lowest saving rates in the world. The average between 1998 and 2004 was about 13.6 percent because of the prevalence of consumer culture promoted by the media. This has held back the growth of the Egyptian economy.

pressure on people to subscribe to Mobinil and don't subscribe to Vodafone. The world's gone mad. Those adverts have to be banned. It's a world of lies and we're exposed to it all day and all night. You walk down the street and you see an ad, turn on the radio and it's adverts. You go home and the television's on, adverts, all of them disgusting and deceitful.

"People act like sheep running after adverts and forking out money all the time, and in the end they tell us the country doesn't have any money. How's that? Then the billions spent on phone talk, where do they come from? Wouldn't it be better if this money was spent on food and housing, education and health? But who can you tell? Since our prime minister was the head of the telephones, that means he's a phone-talk guy.

"But to be honest, the problem's not with the government. The disaster's in the stupidity of people who squander their money on phone calls and tobacco. If they put me in charge of this country for one day, even one minute, the only decree I would issue would be to ban advertisements.

"In the old days, in our day, adverts were meant to serve society, and there weren't so many, there were so few that you had to look high and low to find them, but now the adverts are out to destroy society and they will destroy it and sit on the ruins. Go and say that's what Abu Ismail told you."

Six

I have rarely come across a taxi driver who didn't have experience of working abroad, some of them for long periods in several countries. This driver's experience started in 1977 and continued until 2004, with some breaks, as he said. But as soon as he came home, he would set off again. He had been to Iraq, Kuwait, Saudi Arabia and Libya and had passed through Jordan and Syria of course – real-life experience of one of Egypt's main sources of income, the remittances from Egyptians living, or forced to live, abroad.

The driver was severely critical of the situation in Egypt and told me he had had his fill of empty slogans about loving one's country and nationalist slogans like 'If I were not an Egyptian, I would wish to be one', talk that doesn't take you anywhere or achieve anything. He explained to me that he had been forced to come home two years ago for reasons beyond his control, and that someone under compulsion has a hard time. In his case a hard time meant living now in this filthy country, as he put it. This was nothing unusual to a large extent, held nothing new and was common to a large group of drivers. But he told me stories about exile which were new to my ears, even after close to a quarter of a century listening to these hard-working folk.

"You know the big difference between presidents Sadat and Mubarak?" he said.

Of course I didn't know the real difference and I didn't respond.

"The difference, I tell you, is that Sadat took a great interest in Egyptians abroad. The man really protected us. But Mubarak, he's a coward, he lets the foreign country do us over as it wishes and he doesn't care. I'll tell you a story or two so that you understand the trick (the word 'trick' didn't mean anything at all in this context but that's what he said). In the 1970s Greece brought up the question of Egyptians entering the country by sea and it ended up with the Greeks screaming when they found that the number of Egyptians had greatly increased and that lots of smuggling was going on. So what did they go and do?"

"What?" I asked.

"They showed an Egyptian film, I think it was Abdel Halim Hafez's *My Father Up a Tree*, in several of the cinemas in the districts that had Egyptians. Of course the Egyptians went to see it and half way through the film the police raided the cinemas and picked up the Egyptians one by one, loaded them on to police trucks, then deported them. They put them all on a ship to take them to Alexandria, because most of them were Alexandrians. Who should hear of this but Sadat, and the man went crazy. He spoke to the Egyptian ambassador and told him that as soon as the ship left port he should report it. The ambassador called him back and said: 'The ship's sailed, sir'. Sadat then spoke to the Interior Minister and asked him to pick up 100 Greeks straight away, and instead of deporting them by ship, he had them put on a plane.

"When the Greek prime minister heard the news, he called Sadat, and Sadat told him: 'What you do to my boys, I'll do the same to your boys'. Later he threatened him, said, 'You haven't seen anything yet'. All the Greek prime minister could do was call the ship with the Egyptians on board and tell them to turn around and come back again. All the Egyptians on the boat went back to Athens, and they went and gave them residence permits as well, imagine that, residence. That's a very well-known story. How come you don't know it? That was Sadat, defending every Egyptian abroad."

I told him that, although the story may be well-known, it was the first time I had heard it.

"Well listen to this one," he said, "because there are lots of Sadat stories, but this one's good. There was a tiff between Egypt and the Arab countries after that Camp David business. At the time I was in Iraq. Saddam was turning the world against Egypt and people started to give the Egyptians a hard time, but nothing serious. At the same time there were some, like, skirmishes between Iraq and Iran. The world was on fire. Sadat went and called Saddam and told him: 'Look, young man, politics we can disagree, okay, but if anyone touches one of my boys, no.' And there was a rough neighbourhood where lots of Egyptians lived called Al-Murabbaa in Baghdad. And Sadat went and told him: 'Saddam, I'll set my boys in Al-Murabbaa on you'. Anyway, Saddam understood that some things were one thing, but if Saddam touched a single Egyptian, that was something else.

"But ever since Mubarak came we've been kicked around in every Arab country. Today by the grace of God (at this point he took a sandwich out of the glove compartment and waved it violently in the air) we are humiliated to the utmost humiliation."

When the car stopped, he finished off his rant. "But even so, the best we're humiliated is in our own country, here," he said.

Seven

We drove into Tahrir Square and found it transformed into a military barracks with the arrival of giant riot police trucks and large numbers of officers and policemen. This was about a month after the suicide operation, or the terrorist attack, or the stupid, retarded, desperate attack which led to the death of the attacker and injured some tourists including an Israeli, and which had helped create even more intolerable traffic jams in Cairo.

We turned into Ramses Street and I was surprised to see an endless line of riot police trucks parked on the right-hand side of the street. I looked with sympathy at those wretched policemen, stunted from poor nutrition, their bodies apparently consumed by bilharzia. One of them gave me an imploring look through a small opening like the window of a prison cell. The taxi driver looked at me sarcastically and asked: "Pasha, did you hear the horrible story of what happened to the officer yesterday?"

I said no and he began the story. "They say one of the officers went in to see his troops in one of these trucks (he gestured to the riot police vehicles) and died from the smell." Then the driver burst out laughing. I didn't laugh myself and he carried on. "Can you imagine, sir, the smell of those wretches in this heat when they're packed into the truck like sardines? They keep sweating and farting. The officer, my God, just dropped down dead, he died of asphyxia."

I looked incredulous and asked him: "Did that really happen?"

"Wakey, wakey, it's a joke," said the driver. "You looked grumpy so I thought I'd give you something to laugh about."

"I am a little depressed," I said. "But I hadn't thought it was so obvious."

"Well you don't take anything with you when you go," said the driver. "Well then, listen to this one. A guy was walking through the desert when he found Aladdin's lamp. He rubbed it and a genie appeared and said: 'Hey presto, at your service, your wish is my command.' The guy didn't believe his eyes but went and asked for a million pounds. The genie went and gave him half a million. The guy asked him: 'Okay, so where's the other half? You're going to fleece me from the start?' 'Ah, the government's got a 50-50 stake in the lamp,' the genie replied." The driver burst out laughing again and his laugh made me laugh more than the joke did.

"You know, the government really does take about half of our earnings," the driver said.

"How so?" I asked.

"Various tricks," he said. "Every now and then they dream up a new story. But the best one of all is the seatbelt story."

"What's with the seatbelts?" I asked.

"The seatbelt's a joke," said the driver. "A bad joke and it can only be a trick, a seatbelt for the driver and for the person sitting next to him, like in foreign countries, the bastards. And most people in this country don't drive faster than 30 kilometres an hour, but you know what, business is business.

"Suddenly, just like that, sir, they told you you have to fit a seatbelt and the fine is 50 pounds. Really expensive seatbelts then appear, you can't find one for less than 200 pounds. It's obviously a racket big people are involved in, very big people. Imagine, sir, how many taxis there are in Egypt and how many cars are driving around Egypt without seatbelts. Count it up, that's a job worth millions, the perfect scam."

"Seatbelts are compulsory throughout the world," I said. "You have to fit seatbelts."

"Whadyamean, throughout the world? This is a son-of-a-bitch government. You know, right, that previously the seatbelt counted as a luxury, in other words you had to pay extra customs duty on it. I was importing a Toyota from Saudi Arabia and I had to cut off the seatbelts myself and take out the air-conditioning so that I wouldn't have to pay the luxury customs duty. Then, no more than a few months later, the seatbelt was compulsory. I mean, straight from luxury and extra duty to compulsory. So we ran out and bought seatbelts and they did some good business at our expense.

"The whole story was business on business. The big guys imported seatbelts and sold them and made millions. The Interior Ministry worked on giving out loads of tickets and collected millions. The wretched cops on the street would stop you and say: 'Where's your seatbelt, you bastard?' and you'd have to slip him a fiver, and if he stopped you when an officer was there, it would be 20 pounds. I mean, everyone benefited.

"And after that there's something I want to tell you. I'm sure you know the seatbelt's a lie through and through in the first place. Everyone knows it's for decoration, we fit it just for show." The driver lifted up his seatbelt to show me it wasn't fastened.

"If the police officer stops you, he looks at the belt and he knows very well that it's for decoration. That seatbelt, you have to slam on the brakes to make it grip. But with our cars, when you hit the brakes, the seatbelt comes undone." He laughed aloud. "We live a lie and believe it. The government's only role is to check that we believe the lie, don't you think?"

Eight

"Do you go to the cinema?" I asked him.

"The cinema, ah, it's been a million years since I went to the cinema. Wait a second. I remember the last time I went to the cinema was in 1984. It was Cinema Cairo or the Pigale in Emadeddin Street.

"After that life really minced me up. I came like *faragallah* mincemeat and since then I haven't been to the cinema or the theatre, although I used to go to the cinema often at the end of the 70s. I was living in Geish Street. You know Mahmoud, the guy who sells salted fish?"

"Yes, I know him," I said.

"That's the best place in the world for salted fish."

"And you were living next door?"

"Yes, I was living right next door," the driver said.

"There in Geish Street there was the Hollywood Cinema that used to show five films in the programme – two foreign and one Arabic, then it would repeat the two. We used to watch three films and then the repeats, and other times after the three films were over we would cross the street and on the other side there was Cinema Misr, may it rest in peace and all the others too. That one was both winter and summer. The open-air summer cinema was upstairs. We would pay the man anything and jump over and watch the repeats at Cinema Misr. Those were the days. At that time a ticket was five piastres."

"Do you still remember the films you used to see?"

"There are films one can't forget. My favourite was *Red Sun* with Charles Bronson. Bronson had a look from under his hat, like this, that we would sit and imitate. Remember that film?…How come? In that film he had caught a Japanese guy and he didn't trust him so before they went to sleep he tied his shoes to the laces of the Japanese guy's. The Japanese guy tried to escape. He walked a little, as far as the laces would go – Bronson had let them out a bit – and then he fell down and Bronson woke up.

"As for my favourite Egyptian film, that would be *Bus Driver* with Nour el-Sherif. That I've seen ten times. There was also a great American film, but I don't remember who was in it, called *Duel of the Space Monsters*, and of course *Godzilla* and *The Atomic Monster* and Bruce Lee's *The Big Boss* and the Indian film *Two Friends*. When *White Elephant* came out we went to Cinema Chark in Sayeda Zeinab to see it."

"Didn't you go to the theatre?" I asked.

"What do you mean? I used to go the Vanguard Theatre and we would get tickets for ten piastres. I was just crazy about art. Say what, you a believer?"

"There's no god but God."

"I was part of a theatrical group. It was called the New Revolutionary Group and it was in Galal Street."

"Where's that Galal Street?"

"That's a side street off Emadeddin Street right in front of the Cinema Pigale. One day I was eating *koshari* in Goha's – that's the most famous *koshari* shop in Cairo – and I saw lots of young guys standing around and I found out that they were from the New Revolutionary Group. They told me they were a group from which many very big actors had graduated, like Khairia Ahmed, and they were part of the Ministry of Culture."

"And then?" I prompted.

"I applied to join and starting doing rehearsals. There was one scene where we come into a hotel and sit down and shout out: 'People of God, you here! People of God, you here!' Then they told us as well that we had to bring clothes from home."

I said to myself, this group could never have been part of the Ministry of Culture.

The driver continued: "We had to bring the clothes and the customers too, so I quit."

"And what happened after that?" I asked.

"I don't know what happened. The world changed, or it was me that changed. Say what, you a believer?"

"There is no god but God."

"This is the first time I've spoken about this. I hadn't realised that I haven't seen a film in about 20-something years."

"And all these memories, will they make you go to the cinema again?" I asked.

"Just by chance, I was taking a fare about a week ago to the Sawiris Tower on the river and I heard that a cinema ticket now costs 25 pounds, that means exactly 1,000 times the price only 20 years ago. Imagine, 1,000 times. You know, sir, even the expensive cinemas, until after 1980 the biggest of them was sixteen-and-a-half piastres for a ticket...like Cinema Metro, the Radio, Kasr el-Nil, Cairo and Miami.

"And now most of our cinemas have gone and closed. The Hollywood's turned into something else, the Misr, the Rio in Bab el-Louk, the Star on Kheirat Street, the Isis, the Ahli and the Hilal summer cinema in Sayeda Zeinab, and very many others, have all closed.

"Anyway, what I've seen I've seen and what I haven't seen I might as well not have seen. I've had my time and it's the kids' turn. They've never been to the cinema or the theatre, and they never will. They watch satellite TV at the coffee shop downstairs, God help them. Personally I don't know what will grow in their brains, other than cactus."

Nine

The driver turned the knob to switch the cassette player on. A loud voice came out, warning of women. "My friends in God," it said. "Let us speak today about the temptations which surround us, and there is no doubt that the biggest temptation surrounding Muslims is the temptation of women. O God, we call on you to protect us from the evil of women. The Prophet of God, May God Pray for Him and Grant Him Peace, said that what first tempted the nation of Israel was women, and every nation has a temptation and the temptation of this nation is money, but also women. Women are a great temptation, dangerous to the greatest extent. In fact I used to think that temptations were going to diminish, for in the mid 80s the very short miniskirt appeared, then that fashion faded away in the 1990s and I thought the matter was over. But here it is these days as strong as ever, the like of which the world has never seen.

"Young girls, from 13 to 18 years old, have become the worst thing seen on the face of the earth and, I'm sorry to say, I have learnt from many young men and taxi and minibus drivers that debauchery has spread far and wide and takes place openly, nay visibly, and with the consent of fathers and mothers, husbands and wives. We ask God to take revenge on sinners and to protect young Muslims. It's a disaster, a disaster. Today adornment means nakedness. Girls are wearing T-shirts and trousers as though they were wearing nothing. The Prophet of God, May God Pray for Him and Grant Him Peace, spoke truly when he said: 'Women who are clothed yet naked, their heads like the swaying humps of camels, will neither enter Paradise nor find its fragrance.'

"Oh God, preserve Muslim girls and hide the nakedness of Muslims. It's a disaster, a disaster. The eyes of young men fall left and right on naked bodies, lascivious glances and lewd, wanton laughs, women who are out of control.

"When I go for a walk with young men and the young men say: 'Look, sheikh,' I say: 'I seek God's protection from accursed Satan' but I wonder how any respectable father can allow his daughter to go out of the house dressed like that, as though he were telling her: 'Go out and get yourself debauched.'"

This last sentence from this virtuous sheikh exhausted the very last of my patience and I decided to speak up. "What's this nonsense?" I asked the driver.

"Nonsense! What do you mean, nonsense? Don't say that, sir. That's a lecture by Sheikh Mohamed Hussein Yaaqoub and he's right in every word he says. Girls! They're a plague on us, God protect us. They have all turned into prostitutes, pardon my language. You, sir, don't you walk down the street and see for yourself the red and green they put on their faces, painting themselves with the spirit of the Devil?"

I tried to interrupt him but I failed. He was off and away like a bullet heading for my ear. "Don't be taken in by the *hijab* they wear. Look at their tight trousers and the muck they smear on their faces. And don't let me tell you about the summer and what happens then. God spare us the evil of them. The Arabs come then, sir, and fill the Mohandiseen district. If you look, sir, you'll find the girls like ants on Arab League Street and Batal Ahmed Abdel Aziz Street. A disaster, heaven help us! Those girls need to be slaughtered, no, slaughtering's too good for them, they need to be burned.

"Probably it's one of the signs of the Hour, because the Hour is very near, decadence is spreading and morals are finished, corruption's everywhere, all of these are signs of the Hour."

I despaired of trying to have a conversation with him and decided to confine myself to listening.

"Did you hear, sir, that there are some countries where the number of women is very much greater than the number of men? I don't need to tell you the decadent state those countries are in. That too is a sign of the Hour. The most important thing is the level of the water in the Sea of Galilee. They say that when the Hour comes that lake will have completely dried up, and I hear that already it's drying up and there's only a little water left.

"What's happening in Palestine and Jerusalem, it's perfectly clear. It's only a matter of a few years and it's over. Those who waged *jihad* for God will be taken up to Heaven and the rest will be trodden into the ground, *inshallah*. And all the unscrupulous and the bloodsuckers will go to hell, *inshallah*. And then it will be the women's turn. They'll be roasted in hell until they shout 'Enough'."

I thanked God with all my heart that I had arrived. I fled from the taxi before the driver's curses could reach me, and thanked God that I wasn't a woman, because I could have died of outrage at all the injustice inflicted on me by that man.

I was reminded of Amin Maalouf's beautiful novel *Balthasar's Odyssey*, which is based on historical fact and in which people are awaiting the Year of the Beast, the day the world would end with the appearance of the Antichrist in the year 1666, and they were looking out for signs of the Hour.

Every age has its people who hope that the Day of Resurrection is nigh, to bring them justice against tyranny and oppression.

Ten

The taxi couldn't move for the heavy traffic in Abbas el-Akkad Street in Nasr City. It was nine o'clock in the evening and the shop windows were ablaze with neon lights so bright that I had to close my eyes. Into the taxi from one of the cafes or shops there drifted the voice of the Iraqi singer Kazim al-Saher, singing to the woman he loves.

The driver smacked his lips and sighed. "Poor Iraq! How I grieve for you!" he said.

"Have you been to Iraq by any chance?" I asked him.

"I spent the best years of my life there," he said. "Those Iraqis are the finest people. Even now I can't believe what's happened to Iraq. It's not what I expected at all. Poor Iraq!"

"What did you imagine?" I asked.

"Honestly, I felt that Saddam would beat the Americans. Even when I saw with my own eyes the American tanks rolling down the streets of Baghdad, I told myself that's a plan Saddam has made to draw them into Baghdad and then do a pincer movement on them and wipe them out. Even now I can't believe it. But they're still tough. There's not a day passes that they don't kill some Americans. They'll slaughter them one by one, *inshallah.*"

"May your prayer be answered," I said. "But don't you think that Saddam is the cause of these disasters?"

"To be honest, I like Saddam," the driver said. "He took some really gallant positions on Egyptians. Don't forget that he studied in Cairo. In the 80s when I was in Iraq there were some nasty incidents with Egyptians. But then you found Saddam coming out and making a speech saying any Iraqi who harassed an Egyptian would get six months in jail. Jail straight away, just like that. Frankly, that's a position you can't forget. After that we could walk around Baghdad with our heads held high. Anyway, what happened in Baghdad was official occupation. It's got nothing to do with Saddam or with anything. They said they had dangerous weapons and then they didn't find anything.

"They want their oil, so they went and occupied Iraq. They're a bunch of thieves, along with a bunch of thugs, they turned out the lights and they destroyed poor Iraq.

"But as I was telling you, I know the Iraqis well after living with them for over ten years. They're real men and they'll give the Americans a black eye. It'll only be a matter of months and the bastards will be running away from there with their tails between their legs. They'll save their skins before what happened in Vietnam happens to them there. Believe me, Iraq will be even worse."

"So when did you realise that this wasn't a trick Saddam had pulled and Baghdad really had fallen?" I asked.

"By God, I had hope until they captured Saddam. That day I cried and cried, and I felt that we were being crushed like insects. I felt I was an ant and anyone could squash me. I felt humiliated and I thought of all my friends there and whether they were alive or dead. But I'll tell you one thing, mark my word, it's Iraq that will triumph in the end. What counts is who laughs last, not who laughs at the start."

A burst of optimism lifted my spirits (for a moment).

I got out of the taxi under my apartment and found four young men on the street, smoking Marlboros and drinking Coca-Cola. One of them was wearing Nike trainers and another had a T-shirt with the Stars and Stripes on the left sleeve. The burst of optimism evaporated and I went upstairs to my apartment with my head bowed.

Eleven

Eleven

"If I told you what happened now you wouldn't believe me," said the driver. "I've been driving a cab for 20 years but what happened now was one of the funniest things that ever happened to me."

"Go on then, tell me," I prompted.

"A woman in a face veil stopped me in Shubra and asked me to drive her to Mohandiseen. She got in the back seat and she had a bag with her. As soon as we were out on the Sixth of October Bridge, I saw her looking right and left, and then she went and took the veil off her face. I was watching in the mirror, because, look, I have a small mirror under the big mirror so that I can see what's happening in the back. You have to be on your guard. As the saying goes, better safe than sorry. Anyway, then I found her wearing a headscarf instead. I was surprised but I didn't say anything. A little later she took off her headscarf and she had done her hair in curlers. Then she started undoing the curlers and putting them in her bag. Then she took out a round brush and started combing her hair.

"I looked in the mirror in front of me, and she yelled at me: 'Look in front of you,' she said. 'What are you doing?' I asked her. 'None of your business. You drive and keep your mouth shut,' she shouted back at me.

"Between you and me, I thought of stopping the car and making her get out, but then I thought: 'What's it to me?' So I held out to see what else she would take off. Next thing, I found her taking off her skirt. Nice, I said, we'll have a free view. I looked again and found her putting on a short skirt and thick black tights which didn't show anything. She folded up the long skirt and put it in the bag. Then she started taking off her blouse. My eyes were transfixed on the mirror and when the car in front of me suddenly braked I almost ran into it. She shouted at me like a mad woman: 'Hey, old man, shame on you, keep your eyes on the road.'

"I saw she was putting on a tight blouse and pretty too. Honestly, I didn't answer her. She put the other blouse in the bag and went and started getting out some make-up stuff and started putting on lipstick and rouge on her cheeks. Then she took out an eyebrow brush and started working on her eyebrows. In short, by the time I was coming off the bridge into Dokki she was a completely different woman. Another human being, I tell you, you couldn't say that this was the woman in the veil who stopped me in Shubra.

"She finished off by taking off the slippers she was wearing, taking out a pair of high-heel shoes and putting them on. I told her: 'Look, miss, every one of us has his peculiarities but for God's sake tell me, what's your story?'

"'I'm getting out at Mohieddin Aboul Ezz,' she said. I kept my silence and didn't repeat the question.

"After a while she started telling me her story: 'I work as a waitress in a restaurant there, respectable work. I'm a respectable woman and I do honest work. In this work I have to look good.'

"'At home and in the whole quarter I can't come or go without wearing that veil. One of my friends got me a fake contract to work in a hospital in Ataba and my family think I work there. Frankly, I earn a thousand times as much working here. In a single day I can get in tips what I would earn in one month's salary in the mouldy old hospital.'

"'My friend at the hospital gets 100 pounds a month from me to cover up. She's a girl who looks out for herself. Every day I drop in at her place and get changed. But today it wouldn't have worked to go to her place so I had to take a taxi to change in. Any other questions, Mr Prosecutor?'

"'Lady, I'm no prosecutor, and if I saw one, I'd fall flat on my face. But they say that he who cooks up poison tastes it. You changed in my taxi and I wanted to know why. Once one knows the reason, the wonder ceases,' I said, and thanked her for telling me the story. Now honestly, isn't that a strange story, sir?"

Twelve

I was chatting with the driver and he turned out to be a long-standing fan of Zamalek football club. When he was young he used to go to the stadium to watch Taha Basri, Mahmoud el-Khawaga, Ali Khalil and fresh young players like Hassan Shehata and Farouk Gaafar. This year (this was the winter of 2005) Zamalek was getting beaten by all the teams.

I tried to convert him into an Ahli fan like myself but he told me that Zamalek was in a bad way and kept falling behind so it needed someone to stand by it, not like Ahli, which was up at the top of the league and didn't need anyone to support it. Zamalek was like Egypt, he said, we all have to stand by it so that it stops falling behind.

I asked him how we could stand by Egypt.

"We stand by Egypt if we prepare our children for war," he replied. "It's true that ever since he came to power Mubarak has managed to steer the ship so that Egypt hasn't got into any confrontations with anyone. To be frank, good for him, that's the best thing he's done. The Americans tell us to turn right, we turn right; left, we run to the left. That was important in the past so that we could take a breather and the country's economy could pick up a little and we could stand on our own feet. To be honest, the man has been able to save the country from any recession.

"But war is inevitable. The Israelis won't be able to not make war. Peace will kill them and they know that well. They're itching for a fight. They have their eyes on Syria and Iraq and they keep prodding Iran and they have set Palestine on fire. They want it ablaze so they can get more money from the Americans and they can make their young people more Zionist. If the Jews felt at ease, they would go back to Europe.

"So in the end they will turn on us again, not tomorrow but it will be the day after tomorrow, so everyone's role in the country is to prepare his son for war, because for sure it's coming. We now have to give our army the same spirit with which I fought when I was in the army between 1968 and 1973.

"I have a relative who's an officer in the army, a very clever officer who went to the Soviet Union on training courses. The army's spent a packet on him and sent him abroad several times to make him highly skilled. Know what that officer is doing now?

"He's working at an armed forces mess in Nasr City. What does he do? He organises parties and buys food and serves it. They've turned him into a chef in a restaurant. See the disaster when you take an officer on whom the country has spent thousands of thousands and turn him into a waiter. The disaster is that he's happy and delighted with his status now. How long do you think we'll be able to last without a war?"

"I've no idea," I told him.

"In my opinion no more than another 10 or 15 years," the driver continued. "That means I have a son who's 10 years old and when he leaves university, war will have broken out between us and Israel."

He paused a moment, then resumed: "The problem's with them, not with us. They're the ones who won't be able to keep the peace and it's no use us making peace with ourselves. Peace is something we have to make with someone else, isn't it?"

He laughed at his own joke. "Personally, I'm always explaining the situation to my kids so that when the drums beat, their ears will be ready to heed the call," he added.

Thirteen

As we were driving alongside the Cairo University wall I let slip to the taxi driver how nostalgic I felt for my college days and confessed to him that the dreams for Egypt I dreamt within these walls even now shook me to the core, despite the passage of two decades since my graduation. I said that most of those who sold out had received the keys to the gates, while those who continued to dream had seen their towering hopes dashed to the ground by battering rams.

"And which faculty were you in?" the driver asked.

"Economics and political science," I said.

"So you studied politics, sir?"

"Yes."

"That's great, an excellent opportunity, because for ages I've had a question I wanted to ask," said the driver.

"And what's the question that I can perhaps answer?"

"What would happen if we came and said to America: 'You have nuclear weapons and weapons of mass destruction and if you don't get rid of all these weapons, we will break relations with you and declare war on you, and we will have to use military force to protect Cuba, which is a small country and we have to look after it'?

"Of course, we wouldn't be serious, but we would force the world to take positions. And the world would have to stand with us as they stood with them when they said the same thing against Iraq, and as they are now saying against Iran. I'm not saying we would fight them. Of course you definitely understand me. But we would say exactly the same thing as they are saying to the countries of the world. I mean, for example, we'd ask to monitor the American elections because we're not confident their election procedures are sound, we'd ask for there to be international monitoring of the ballot boxes, and anyway we would have the right to say that, 'cause everyone in America and the whole world said there was fraud in the Bush elections and that his brother in his state fixed the elections and made him win. And we'd say we have to defend democracy and we have to send Egyptian judges from here to make sure the democratic process is proper.

"You know if we did that, we'd make them understand what they are doing to people, and we'd vent some of the anger that's inside us, just like when some disaster happens and there's nothing to be done and you let off steam to whoever and you find yourself calmed down, but the disaster's still the same as it was.

"Or else we could sue America for supporting international terrorism and taking sides with countries that aren't democratic, and get evidence of that and, as you know, it's very easy to get evidence, especially in such a matter. Then when you make this move, you're on the side of democracy and against terrorism and you'll find a few countries taking your side against America.

"We could also call for economic sanctions against America if they don't comply, I mean take what their secretary of state Rice says every day to all the poor countries in the world and say the same thing to their faces.

"The most important thing is that all of us should cancel out what the Americans say. We should say 'White Irish Protestant American', or 'Black Muslim American', or 'Hispanic American', or 'White Catholic American', or 'Black

Protestant American', just like they say these days: 'six Iraqi Shi'ites died and two Iraqi Sunnis', and the sons of bitches at our newspapers repeat the same thing, and of course you find them saying: 'an Egyptian Christian' and 'an Egyptian Muslim', and of course we have to demand as loud as we can the right to defend the rights of the blacks in America, and sue if some White Scottish American kills some Black African American, of course we have to make a big scene at least because he's African like us, I mean, he's much more closely related to us than a White Italian American with freckles is to some Egyptian Christian, I mean, protecting the rights of the black minority there, that's our role, and we have to intervene in everything big and small.

"I know I always talk too much and repeat myself. I'm waiting for you to respond but you just hold your tongue and don't respond."

"I'm thinking about what you're saying," I answered.

"You see, I leave the radio on all day, and every day what the Americans say gets up my nose. It's enough to drive a man out of his senses. It's very serious because soon people will explode. 'We feed you, we put you on your potty, do this, don't do that.' Soon we'll burst and that'll be the end of it. So I had this idea, that we should do to them just as they do to us. People who live in glass houses shouldn't throw stones. And those people live in houses of cracked glass mixed with cancer."

"Okay so why don't you send that suggestion to..." I started.

"I'm just letting off steam, man, I mean shooting the breeze. They're ready to let the Americans do anything to us. The suggestion they might like is the Americans put a camera in every Egyptian house so they can monitor the population explosion."

Fourteen

This time the driver was Nubian and it's very rare that you come across a Nubian taxi driver in Cairo. That's very strange. Why don't Nubians work as taxi drivers? Especially since they work as drivers in companies or for private individuals, embassies or international organisations. I don't know the reason but the question does call for thought.

He was a young Nubian and I learnt from him that he had come to Cairo recently and was trying to settle down here. I sat explaining to him the topography of the city: "Yes, turn right here in to Sharif Street, you know that Sharif, he was the grandfather of Queen Nazli, and after that right and right again into Sabri Pasha, who was minister of justice in the days when they used to say: 'Keep to the straight and narrow and you'll confound the enemy', straight on in to Suleiman Pasha Square, the statue is of Talaat Harb, but after 50 years we still call the square and the street Suleiman Pasha, who was Suleiman the Frenchman who came to Egypt and set up the modern Egyptian army with Mohamed Ali and his son Ibrahim. Here in Egypt the state goes and changes the names of streets and nobody knows about it. A year passes, or ten or 50, and people stick to the old names. That's Antikhane

Street and that's Champollion. They've changed the names of all those, but the government's on one planet and we're on another, and I don't know and nobody knows what their new names are, which they have had for going on 50 years, but never you mind, those Aswan people are the nicest there are."

"God preserve you," said the driver. "You're too kind, sir."

"And where in Aswan are you from?" I asked.

"I mean, I was between Aswan itself and Abu Simbel."

"And you were working there?" I asked.

"I was dabbling in everything, and after that I worked a little on the Toshka land reclamation project."

"Really! That's the national project of our times!"

"No, it's not national or anything. That's a project that's dead and buried."

"What do you mean, dead?" I asked him.

"We had very great hope in it and we felt that the world was going to smile on us, but unfortunately it's all over. And what brought me to Cairo is that there's nothing doing there, it's over," he said.

"If what you say is true, then it's a disaster."

"What you say is 100 per cent right. For us as people living there, the project sucks, I mean, to be honest, there's no work there for us. But why do you say a disaster, God forbid? The world has its ups and downs, swings and roundabouts. There's no disaster or anything."

"No, of course it's a disaster. Egypt has spent billions on the project," I said.

"Billions...Okay, why didn't they share out that money to people? Aren't there 70 million of us, that makes about 10 million families. They could have given each family a thousand pounds. We would have said prayers of thanks for the government till the day we died. And haven't you noticed that even in the papers there's no longer anything about it? Once news about Toshka used to pour out at you from every tap you opened. Now even if you turn on the shower, you won't find a single drop of water about Toshka."

"And how long have you been in Cairo?" I asked.

"Three months. We came, eight guys together, and we hired a room in Boulak el-Dakrour for 80 pounds a month, that's ten pounds each. And at the coffeeshop I got to know the owner of this car. I've always driven and I'd got myself a licence to work as a driver just in case. I did some paperwork and proved I was resident here in Cairo. I take the car from him for one shift a day."

"How much do you pay him for the shift?" I asked.

"Sixty pounds. The car's good, as you can see. He's trying me out, and I hope it will all work out."

"Are you planning to stay in Cairo?"

"What kind of question is that? What would make me want to go back there?"

Fifteen

We were standing in front of the New Ramses College in Ahmed Lutfi el-Sayed Street, where my children go to school, and the street was crowded. There was a large number of public buses pumping tonnes of exhaust fumes into my face and I was close to suffocating from the level of pollution around me. I asked myself what my beloved Cairo must be doing to the lungs of her inhabitants. I saw a taxi approaching me and it came to a stop as if in joy at finding a customer. I got in without saying where I was going, as I usually would. I found the driver smoking a cigarette and blowing the smoke in my face.

I couldn't bear the sight of this trail of smoke, dancing through the air towards my gills like a poisonous snake. My lungs sent my brain a strongly worded message to act immediately to stop the sight of this silent dance of smoke. I thought a moment and realised that if I asked him politely to put out his cigarette, out of kindness for my chest, he would arrogantly dismiss my request, so I decided to try out the tough silent approach on the chance that for a moment he might imagine that I was a police officer and might submit to my authority and throw away the cigarette.

"Throw that cigarette away," I said to him sternly. "Isn't it enough the filth we already breathe?"

He looked me over carefully, put my face on one scale and the face of a police officer on another and began to compare the weight of the two in his mind's eye. Then he threw the cigarette out of the window and I realised that my face could pass for that of a policeman.

"Go to Agouza," I said, continuing to play the tough guy role.

"Sure," said the driver.

I knew that if I uttered a single word more, the cat would be out of the bag and the driver would start smoking again, so I stayed silent.

"Whatever you say, sir. But say, you a believer?"

"There is no god but God," I answered.

"I used to work for a millionaire and my salary was 700 pounds a month, leaving aside the gifts, the clothes, the holiday bonuses and so on. I gave up that cushy life because I wasn't allowed to smoke. I work as a taxi driver all day long and do whatever I can to stay free and smoke at my leisure, but for your sake I threw the cigarette away. And that was a Marlboro, I tell you."

"May you live long," I said.

"Because I started smoking late, I mean when I was like in secondary school, and after that I went into the army from 1973 to 1976. At that time they used to give out cigarettes to us for free, every soldier one pack a day. Those cigarettes were a gift from Gaddafi, from Libya I mean, for the Egyptian warriors. Before the army I didn't use to smoke much, I mean just every now and then. When I was at secondary school, my family didn't know I smoked, and after I graduated from the army a pack of Marlboro cost forty-three-and-a-half piastres and Egyptian cigarettes were between 15 or 20 piastres. That's when I started smoking Marlboro, and Marlboro now cost seven pounds fifty and Cleopatra cost two pounds fifty, I mean devastating, but what can you say, they're a pleasure to smoke.

"Well I'll tell you a very strange story. I'm from Assiut in the south and my family told me 'That's enough' and I have to get married.

"I told them okay. They said, 'No, you have to marry a local girl.' They took me there and we went and met a girl I'm related to. And, as one does in Cairo, I took a cake with me. Of course, that's something that doesn't happen there. I went in with the cake and they were very surprised, but I don't know what happened. I didn't take to the girl, there was no chemistry between us, so I took my leave and they understood. They went and sent the cake to my uncle's house because my father had been living in Cairo for ages and I don't have anywhere to live there. And as I was going home, I met my cousin in my other uncle's house and the chemistry worked. It attracted me to her and her to me and we got on well. My folks couldn't believe it and before a couple of days were up we were getting engaged. She was a beautiful girl and working at a primary school there.

"I came back to Cairo and sat thinking. 'Look lad,' I said, 'If you marry her, you'll add to your expenses', and what I bring in isn't enough to make ends meet in the first place. Where will I find the money for my smokes, and my hashish? No offence, sir, but we only smoke a joint once a week.

"I sat turning the question over in my mind and I found that if I married her I would have to give up smoking and give up my hashish. Because I can see what those around me are doing. So I went off to the country after my folks and broke off the engagement, and ever since I've not repeated any of that business.

"I live free, smoke at my leisure, roll a joint at my leisure, don't owe nothing to no one. Why don't you have a cigarette, sir? They're Marlboro, look at the packet here."

Sixteen

Sixteen

The driver's features had an unfathomable sadness, a sadness that had spread until it engulfed him, as though the cares of the world had accumulated and clumped together, eventually forming a heavy ball that descended on the soul of this wretch. Just to look at him was enough to show that some disaster had befallen him.

I asked him the reason for his deep sadness. "Really I don't know what to do or how to cope. My brain never stops churning it over and I can't make a decision. I'm going to go crazy. I feel like my brain is going to explode," he replied.

"What's the matter then?" I asked.

"The story is that I have a school run. I take six kids and the kids pay just 80 pounds a month. Two days ago the father of two, a boy and a girl, went to jail or was arrested, I don't know exactly. Yesterday I went to get my monthly money and their mother told me what happened and asked me to wait until he's safely out.

"To be profitable a school run has to be seven or eight kids and I have six. At the same time what will the boy and the girl do? Their mother wears the face veil and doesn't go out of the house. My wife tells me: 'This is work, and work is work.

Tell her that either she pays or you don't drive the kids to school.' And their mother swears to me blind that she doesn't have money to eat and that patience is the key to salvation, and that if you do good on Saturday you'll have your reward on Sunday.

"I don't know what to do. My conscience tells me I have to drive the kids to school and at the same time I'm a poor soul who needs someone to throw him a bone. I will definitely lose money on the school run. What do you think, sir?"

"It's very hard for me to have an opinion on that," I told him. "Someone with his hand in the water is not like someone with his hand in the fire."

"No, honestly, if you were in my place, what would you do?" he asked.

"My view is do what's right and forget about it, and drive the kids to school."

"My father, may he rest in peace, always used to say do good deeds and they will come back to you, like a sound and its echo, if you don't shout out loud you won't hear the echo. Likewise, if you don't do right by people wholeheartedly then it will never come back to you. May he rest in peace, my father, but he was living in a different time, a time when he used to come home from work at three o'clock in the afternoon and stay sitting with us. I see my kids once a week, if I see them.

"Okay, so if I drive the kids to school this month and their father doesn't come out of prison, how long should I wait? It's no use having to do good deeds forever. Because my wife kicked up one helluva fuss when I told her yesterday I would drive them to school and to hell with it. Besides to be honest I really like the girl Amina. She's five years old and looks just like my sister's daughter Asma. A beautiful girl, funny and quiet. Ever see a girl who's naughty and quiet at the same time? Ah, that's Amina for you. I really don't know what to do."

As I got out I told him to take whatever decision he wanted and stick to it, and not to think about it after that.

He took the fare from me and didn't even look at it. His state of mind when we parted was hardly better than it was when we met.

Seventeen

Seventeen

The pyramids of Giza are the only surviving wonder of the ancient world, a model of splendour and perfection, a marvel and a prodigy. Fouad the driver, with his towering frame thinner than a cane, was also one of the seven wonder drivers of the world. He was a taxi driver, a specialist in the stock exchange, a venerable speculator, a star of stars and the focus of attention of his relatives and friends because he had made some of them rich in a matter of days. He monitored with the eyes of a hawk, as he would put it, any movement in any share. The world of the stock exchange and share movements was his first world, followed in second place by the taxi world.

"The stock exchange is not gambling, it's an adventure, I mean there's only one letter difference between the two words in Arabic. You know, once it gets in your blood, it will never come out. Much harder than giving up smoking," said Fouad.

"So why don't you take it up full-time? Because a jack of all trades is the master of none," I asked him.

"I only have a mind for one and that's for the stock exchange. Driving a taxi doesn't call for a mind, it just takes experience and I'm an expert. Besides, driving's in my blood and it's my original job, which puts bread on the table, and this car is my car, I don't rent it. But the money I make on the stock exchange is like pocket money. Driving earns your daily bread if you don't have money to pay for the dessert. It's great to have dessert but what matters most is to eat in the first place. If you have it, eat dessert. But the stock exchange money isn't guaranteed. The market can take you up suddenly and then suddenly slam you down on the ground.

"For example, I play with the money of 20 of my friends and relatives. I took a sum from each of them ages ago and after that we meet at the coffee shop and I sit and tell them what I'm going to do. And then there's trust. They give me money without receipts or anything. The most important thing is trust, the account at the brokerage is in my name only," he said.

"What do you mean, your account at the brokerage? I don't know anything about this game at all," I asked him.

"Look, to cut a long story short, you have to go first of all to open an account in your name. Your name is coded, that's what they call it, coded, that means it's registered at Misr Clearing company. Then you see what you want to buy and sell and you tell your broker. I go and look at the stock market screen in one of the stock exchange rooms in Bourse Street downtown and I see how the market is moving and I buy and sell. In the evening I go to an internet café to websites that give you the prices, but a quarter of an hour delayed, like arabfinance.com. You put in the code for the company for which you want to know the price and away you go."

"So you're quite the expert," I said.

"Ask me anything, because everyone comes and asks me what to buy and what to sell."

"And do you make money for them?" I asked.

"Believe me, the other day we were all of us ruined, last Tuesday it was, a day not to forget, it was March 14. I usually drive early in the morning and at midday I go see what's news. I found the stock market was collapsing. I had bought shares in two companies for my group – Oriental

Weavers and Ezz Steel – and I found the shares kept falling. Oriental Weavers I had bought for 83 pounds and right in front of my eyes it kept dropping till it hit 61 pounds. I thought it would carry on falling. I found Ezz Steel, which I had bought at 79 pounds, had fallen to 55 pounds. I thought: 'We're instantly ruined. For sure the market's collapsed and prices will keep going down.' I thought: 'I'll get out injured rather than lose my shirt. I sold at a loss of about 30 per cent and that day I was playing with about 30,000 pounds. I lost about 9,000 pounds in two hours.

"I found my knees were shaking and I couldn't stand up straight. I sat down at the coffee shop and felt that I was going to die. And then I went to sleep. When I woke up, I found that prices had gone back up to where they were. Frankly, I laughed and applauded the master who played the market right. The dinosaurs are dinosaurs and the flies are flies. I'm flies and I buzz around in order to live but that day I learned that I was playing with fire.

"When the prices fell, we all sold. Did anyone buy? You tell me, who bought? I tell you, of course – the people who know that prices won't fall any more and will go back up. Where did they get the information so that they bought? Those are the big fish that the country stands behind. Look, when the share falls about 20 pounds and you have the info, then you step in and buy a million shares, remember that every one of these companies has over 50 million shares. And at the end of the day the share's gone back to its original price and you go and sell, then you've earned 20 million pounds in three hours. Good business. In a single day they wiped out the flies who fled from the massacre and they made money for the few very big fish. What have you been writing down there?"

"I'm writing down the numbers you keep telling me. You've overwhelmed me with numbers," I said.

"What, you want to play as well?" asked Fouad. "Hand over your money and I'll add you to my group."

"I'm not one for gambling or adventure. And between you and me, I think it's both gambling and adventure. I also think you should submit your resignation from this business as long as the big fish are feeding."

"But that's the way of the world," said Fouad. "For the big fish to get fat, we flies mustn't stop buzzing, or how else would they get fat?"

Eighteen

I was invited with my twin sons, Bahaa and Badr, to lunch
with our friend Sahar, and the three of us were in high
spirits, in my case because Sahar is an exceptional cook,
Bahaa and Badr because they were looking forward to seeing
her sons. We got in a taxi and set off.

The driver examined me thoroughly, then looked at my
sons sitting in the back. I examined him too. He was a large
man, like the trunk of a sycamore tree sitting beside me. His
head brushed the roof of the car and the steering wheel was
like a small child's toy in his hands. His face was as if carved
from stone.

"Your kids of course?" said the driver.

"Yes, my kids."

"God preserve them, a blessing from God," he said.

"God preserve you."

"God protect them for you."

"God protect you."

"How old are they?" he asked

"They'll be 10 in a few months," I told him.

"God give them a long life," he said.

I didn't answer because I had grown tired of this scratched

record which might not end. But after a short silence, the driver continued.

"I have a son too," he said.

"God bless him for you."

"God be praised, God be praised. He was a gift from Our Lord. Because after I got married, we discovered there was a problem having children. We kept running here and there until after seven years Our Lord favoured us and we had Hussein. I called him Hussein after Our Master Hussein so he'll walk in his footsteps.

"But alas (and here the driver let out a heartfelt, broken sigh), when he was four we discovered he had cancer, and now he's lying in the Cancer Institute, and you can't imagine how much I've spent on him in medical fees. It's really exorbitant. I've run round everywhere to raise the money. I begged from the mosque and, God reward them, they gave me money, but it wasn't enough. Some of the guys told me to go to the church and I told them 'But I'm Muslim.' They told me to go anyhow. I went and gave them the medical reports, and they too, God reward them, went and gave me some money. I keep begging from everyone around me but it's no good, his treatment costs more. His mother couldn't take it and now she has heart trouble and she's staying at the Heart Institute as well."

"Good heavens!" I said. "These things are surely sent to try us."

"God be praised for everything," the driver continued. "God keep your boys for you, God protect them for you."

"Thanks," I said. "And how are your son and your wife doing now?"

"God preserve us all. When I go to visit him (another heartfelt sigh) in the institute, I find him jumping for joy and shouting out 'My father's here, my father's here.' I tell you, it wrenches my heart out of my rib cage. When I hug him and take him in my arms, I say 'Lord, ordain that he survive.' (He said this sentence in a sobbing tone) And his mother, I don't know what to do for her. She has to have a heart operation. Anyway, God be praised for everything."

Then he looked at my boys. "God preserve them for you," he said.

Then he looked at me, a look that implored compassion.

I'm used to drivers of this sort, drivers who work hard to arouse your sympathy so that you give them more money. But this man had a deep effect on me, although I was certain he was probably lying and his story was completely fabricated from start to finish for the sake of a generous bonus at the end of the trip. But I was moved nonetheless. I don't know why I was moved. Possibly because of his magnificent performance, or because he was as big as a sycamore tree, possibly because an inner apprehension told me that there was a possibility, however slight, that he was telling the truth. Anyway, in the end his bonus was a contribution to the Cancer Institute, the Heart Institute and any other institute he might imagine.

Sitting at Sahar's house, I twitched my nose and a smoky bouquet of meat, onions and cinnamon wafted by, even permeating the pores of my skin. I felt in a state of peace and I told Sahar my story with the driver. She wasn't surprised.

"That's a story that's repeated often. That must have happened to me a hundred times. We've become a nation of beggars. You've never heard that?" she said.

"No."

"Anyone who didn't go to prison in the time of Abdel Nasser will never go to prison. Anyone who didn't get rich in the time of Sadat will never get rich. Anyone who hasn't begged in the time of Mubarak will never beg," she added.

"Then count me a beggar and bring me anything to eat. I'm dying of hunger."

Nineteen

Nineteen

It was Giza Street and it looked like the Day of Resurrection. The taxi wasn't moving, and the pollution combined with the tedium made time stand stiflingly still. The Faculty of Medicine was on my left and the Zoo on my right, the line of cars stretching endlessly in front of me and behind. I estimated I would reach Cinema City on Pyramids Street in two centuries' time.

I had no desire for conversation with the driver, for silence was indispensable to complete the circle of pollution and boredom. But in the end the driver decided to break the barrier of silence.

"I had a guy who got out a while back who told me the Khan el-Khalili bombing wasn't the work of the Islamists at all, but that the government did it so people will sympathise with them against the Islamists before the presidential elections. And for your information more than one person has told me the same story. What do you think, sir?" he asked.

"I think that's nonsense," I said. "A perversion of the facts and offensive. More than once over the past 30 years the Islamists have carried out such terrorist attacks, which do harm to society and to themselves, and they keep on doing it and you can't see why and you can't see who's behind it or who's financing it. So what do you think?" I said.

"The government is weak, they don't know how to do things like that," he said. "If they could plan that carefully we wouldn't be in the state we're in. To pull off political operations of that kind, you have to have daring and courage, and the planning must be sound. We wretches don't know how to do it. Now if it was the Israeli government, then they could think. But us? No, impossible."

"You mean you think that carrying out dirty attacks on civilians shows strength? What kind of talk is that?" I said.

"Politics has always been dirty," he said. "We all know that the Americans hit the Twin Towers in New York and pinned it on the Islamists. In politics the motto is 'If it works, try it.' And we're going into elections, and that means every trick is allowed. The government has to make the Islamists look like shit so people will say they are ruining the economy more than it's already ruined."

"What are you talking about?" I said. "Are there no morals? Is there no law? Is there no constitution? You think we live in the jungle?"

"Why? Where do you think we live, in a city? A jungle would be a relief compared with where we are. You know where we live?"

"Where?" I asked.

"In Hell."

Twenty

The parliamentary elections had ended, for better or for worse, after the usual disasters owing to acts of violence. The outcome was the disappearance of all Egyptian opposition parties from the left to the right or, in short, the appearance of two opposing forces: the government and the Muslim Brotherhood, or as the newspapers called them, the outlawed Brotherhood group.

"It has to stay outlawed," said the driver, "so they can pick them up at any time if the Brothers try to push their luck. They have to stay behind the line drawn for them and if they lose their cool and get close to the line they'll be arrested. I'll tell you a very funny thing that happened in Tunis, because my wife's Tunisian. One day Ben Ali came, the Tunisian president, and said the elections would be free and democratic, and he made all the mice come out of their holes. He went and had elections, and just a few days later he went and arrested all the Islamists and anyone who'd gone and voted for the Islamists. Ever since then they haven't come out of their holes. See the beauty of it. In one free election, he managed to wrap it all up.

"Here I think the Brotherhood don't intend to cross the red line and they are playing the game the right way.

"But frankly, even if they weren't standing in all the constituencies, they gave the National Democratic Party a hard time. The government had to cheat in several constituencies, like in Dokki with Amal Osman. Hazem Salah Abu Ismail was ahead of her, he was winning, and in the end they fiddled it and made Amal Osman win. Like what happened in Madinet Nasr with Sallab and several other constituencies as well.

"Because I'm originally from Fayoum, Youssef Wali country, and there the National Party couldn't do a thing. The Brotherhood swept the board.

"But frankly, in our elections there's a boss who fixes everything properly and everyone stays within the bounds set for them, and so we look like a country that's 100 per cent really democratic. But you know what the truth is?"

"What?" I said.

"There's no democracy in any country in the world," he continued. "Of course in our case there's no question about it, but also abroad. In America people go to vote for two parties but in reality they are one and the same, as if here you were to go and vote for either Mubarak or Mubarak. They are the same party with two names. And in Europe it's the same story, they all look like each other. The difference between us and them isn't in democracy, because that's an illusion and exists only in books, but the difference is in the law. They have laws that are enforced, while we don't. That's the difference.

"Over there it's no good them saying the Muslim Brotherhood is outlawed and then having the Muslim Brotherhood the only ones standing against the National Democratic Party. Over there outlawed means outlawed, while here it's outlawed and they let them operate. By the way, that's not just the Brotherhood. By law any one of us can be arrested, anyone.

"For example if they stopped me now they would ask for the licences. If the licences are okay they would ask for the fire extinguisher. I'd get it out for them and they would say it's too far away from you, or it's empty or too old. Of course you couldn't see how he knew it was empty or too old. If you get further, they'll say the stickers. Of course every car puts things on the mirrors and that's against the rules. If you get beyond that, they'll say safety and roadworthiness, and for sure every car in Egypt has some small dent on it somewhere.

"So in short he has a million ways to arrest you, even if everything's in order and he just doesn't like your face. He can investigate, and in the end he has the emergency law that has been around for a quarter of a century. I tell you, if they went into any house in the land of Egypt they could dig out illegal things by the score, because with us the law's as flexible as a big rubber band.

"In other words we're all outlawed, and anyone in this country is in the same position as the Brotherhood. They can be picked up at any time, God protect us."

Twenty-one

Fish

"God forgive me but I don't pray," said the driver. "I don't even go to the mosque. I don't have time. I work all day long. Even fasting, it's a day here and two days there. I can't work without smoking. But I'd seriously like to see the Brotherhood come to power. Why not? It looks like everyone wants them after the parliamentary elections."

"But if they came to power and found out you don't pray, they'd string you up by the ankles," I told him.

"No, because I would pray in the mosque in front of everyone."

"Why do you want them to come to power?" I asked.

"Because we have tried everything," he said. "We tried the king and he was no good. We tried socialism with Abdel Nasser, and even at the peak of socialism we still had pashas from the army and the intelligence. After that we tried the political centre and then we tried capitalism but with government shops and a public sector and dictatorship and emergency law, and we became Americans and little by little we'll turn into Israelis, and it's still no good, so why don't we try the Brotherhood and maybe they will work out, who knows?"

"You mean just as an experiment?" I said. "You can try wearing a big pair of trousers or a tight shirt, but it's no good experimenting with the future of a country."

Milk
"They say a man with one eye will hit you in the eye, and then the Americans are quite impossible to understand. They help President Mubarak, they help the Brotherhood and they help the Christians who are causing trouble abroad. They pay money to the Saudis, who give it to the Islamists who carry out terrorist operations with it against America, say. It's a major mess and enough to baffle anyone. But again I tell you that we have to try out the idea of the Brotherhood taking power for a while and see what they'll do. That way we would have some new faces, and as you know a new sieve is tighter and maybe that sieve would pull our economy together a little.

"Talking of the economy, have you heard this joke?"

"No," I said.

Tamarind
"They say the Egyptian economy is like a prostitute's knickers. As soon as she pulls them up they come down again," he said. Then he burst out laughing.

Twenty-two

"All the trials and tribulations that have fallen on our heads are nothing compared to what's happened in Iraq," the driver said.

"People ask you 'Do you know so-and-so?' You say yes. Have you lived with him? No. Then you don't know him. Now I've lived with those Iraqis for years and they don't at all deserve what's happening to them.

"I was living in Hurriya City in Iraq, in the district with the officers' quarters. I was working then as a salesman in a shop. The system there is that every shop has a room for living in. You wouldn't believe the people there. My first Ramadan there I was with two Egyptians, sitting and preparing the meal for the end of the fast, and suddenly there was a knock on the door. I opened it and found the neighbours had sent us a large tray with the evening meal. I told them, 'We already have our meal ready, God be praised.' They said, 'Have some for the road.' You wouldn't believe the tray. We had to open both halves of the door to get it through. One person couldn't carry it on his own. It took two. And the other half of the door was jammed and they stood there waiting. The tray had everything on it, even cold water with ice. And they kept sending us that tray for the 30 days of Ramadan, bowls and bowls of food every day.

"Over there, friends are real friends. Once I was travelling to Cairo and I had a friend called Karim who worked with security at the airport. I found he came over to my place and it was him who woke me up and I found him bringing me breakfast, and he had a car to take me to the airport and he stayed with me until he got me on the plane.

"And another friend of mine was working in intelligence and he had a grocer's next to my house. My God, he bent over backwards to help me. They're really fine men and anyone who tells you otherwise is a liar.

"If it was up to me, I'd like to go and fight with them. I feel like a bastard. I was with them in the good times and now I'm far away in the bad times. Yet I'm not a bastard but there's no way I can do anything. God damn the bastards, their day will come, *inshallah*."

Twenty-three

It is very rare that one meets a driver like this one. A man in his 50s, elegantly dressed, close-shaven, smelling of after-shave, with a deep calm voice like a Buddhist priest or an ascetic in the desert or maybe a saint in a remote monastery.

His immaculate taxi took us past the front of Cairo University and we talked about the ugly buildings that had been built in front of the Faculty of Commerce and the Faculty of Economics and Political Sciences.

"Everything in this world has its beauty," he said. "You only have to open your heart to see the beauty around you. But if you're like most people and you've closed your heart, how can you see the light shining around you? We in Egypt are truly blessed, one of the most beautiful and greatest countries in the world and you live here. And when you open your heart, you'll see unbelievable things in Egypt. Because the Nile is enough. Just as it gives us water to drink and food to eat, the Nile can also wash our souls. Looking at it cleanses your heart.

"For the past 30 years, I've divided my day into three shifts. One shift I drive the taxi, one shift I sit with my wife and kids, and one shift I sit fishing in the Nile and wash my spirit and my body and my eyes. In the book of the Nile I read the words of Our Lord. After those four hours I feel that I'm transparent and that Our Lord is with me and holding my hand so that I fear only Him. If everyone in the country sat and looked at the book of the waters, our life would be something else altogether. There would be no bribery or corruption because someone with a pure heart cannot do anything wrong.

"Every day I finish the taxi shift worried, worried for my children, worried about the future, worried about the world, and after I finish the fishing shift I'm full of hope, hope for tomorrow, and confidence that everything will be fine and that Our Lord won't forget us. Because Egypt's mentioned in the Koran and we are God's soldiers, so how could He forget us? Impossible."

He was speaking to me in his deep mellow voice, a voice much like that of the matriarch of the Abdel Rasoul family in Shady Abdel Salam's film *The Mummy*. His voice did not seem to come from the person speaking, but rather direct from Almighty God, words of deep meaning that came from the heart, a real belief in the essence of real things and not in their artificial appearance.

I will always remember this handsome man whenever I contemplate the book of the Nile, and I will always remember that after every worry comes a feeling of hope for a better tomorrow.

Before I got out I asked him his name, and that too I will remember: Sharif Shenouda.

Twenty-four

In his appearance, the type of shoes he wore, the brand of his glasses, this young man was different from the mainsteam of taxi drivers. His car too was a make different from all the other taxis I have ridden, because taxis generally don't go beyond a limited number of models, all rear-wheel drive. The most common of them are the Shahin, the Lada, the Fiat 1400 and 1500, the Peugeot 504. Then there are the newer cars that came on to the market after the idea of bank loans for taxis appeared in the mid 90s: the Skoda, the Suzuki Swift, which they call the Suzuki Zift or 'rubbish', and the Hyundai.

But this car was as different as its driver.

"What make is this car? I asked him.

"This is a Toyota Cressida," he said.

"It's not very common."

"It's common in the Gulf, because it's a little expensive. It's 2000cc and comes with air-conditioning and central locking, even the tape deck is original, see what's written on it: 'Toyota'."

"No, it's a beautiful car. The most important thing about it is it's wide. Have you being working long as a driver?"

"No, no," he said firmly. "I'm not a driver. I'm a graduate of the Faculty of Commerce and now I'm doing my master's, and I work as an accountant in a pharmaceutical company, but in the afternoon I take the taxi for some extra income."

"Why? Are you married or what?"

"I married young," he said. "Marriage of course is ordained by God. And I had children early too. You know, money and children are the ornament of life in this world, and of course on my salary we can't live."

"If you don't mind my asking, how much do you earn?"

"I get 450 pounds a month and that's a good salary. I have colleagues who get 350. I'm a good accountant, but the money just doesn't last the month. I did an Excel spreadsheet with the household expenses and I discovered it's a puzzle that even Bill Gates couldn't solve. I pay 120 pounds rent and the gas, electricity and the doorman make another 30 pounds. That leaves us 300, because it's hard to live with today's prices. We need 30 pounds a day, of course for me and my wife, not to forget Islam and Suha, obviously that's including the food and transport, clothes and medicine and the unexpected expenses that come up every month from heaven knows where. That means the rest of the salary is gone in 10 days. I don't need to tell you what the milk bill does to my salary. Obviously the two kids have to drink milk, and their mother after being pregnant twice got severe calcium deficiency and the doctor told her she had to drink milk. You wouldn't imagine that I spend 100 pounds a month on milk, because a litre costs 3.25. Of course you might tell me that milk's for rich people, and you're right, but I don't know why the missus is so insistent on it. She tells me she and the kids must drink milk every day. With her there's milk and then there's everything else.

"But really, it's not just milk, everything's got so expensive. A kilo of beans has gone up to three pounds, or the government cooking oil, a litre costs 3.50. I don't need to tell you about the corn oil and those things, a litre of that has gone up to six pounds.

"In other words it's impossible for anyone in Egypt to make

do with his salary. Because how much are salaries? From 300 to 600 pounds and no more than that. And that's not enough. So what's the answer? Either we steal or take bribes or work all day. I work from eight in the morning until four at the company. Then I go and take the taxi from five o'clock until one o'clock in the morning, because from the company to the owner's place takes about an hour on public transport. I get home about two in the morning, have dinner and go to bed.

"God be praised that I don't have to beg from anyone. It's going well and in just a few years my salary will go up, and after I get the master's, *inshallah*, my salary will go up again. Young people have to slave at the start, and later take it easy, *inshallah*."

He was speaking about his hope for a bright future with such certainty that I worried for him. I hope the hand of fate takes pity on him, for this man deserves it.

Twenty-five

"How will we do in the final of the Africa Nations Cup?" I asked him. "Will we win, or will Ivory Coast?"

"I'm not really big on football, but I hope we win," he said.

"Haven't you been watching the matches?"

"This African championship isn't ours, it's only for rich people. There's no need for us any longer. In the last match, the semi-final, my son begged me to get him a ticket because he's crazy about football. I tried to get him a third-class ticket but it was impossible. Then we found out that the driver of some guy at the Football Federation is selling them on the black market. It got to the stage that people were joking that someone found Aladdin's lamp and asked the genie for a ticket to the Egypt match, and the genie answered him: 'No, for God's sake make a wish that's a little easier.' I tried to get the kid a black market ticket and I found one for 200 pounds. Imagine, third class for 200, and second class up to 300 pounds, and first class was over 500.

"That means a ticket was one month's salary, so I'm telling you it's a championship only for the rich, like they put on films 'For Adults Only'. But in this championship it's 'For the Very Rich Only'.

"Have you seen the spectators on television? They all look like Europeans. They have blonde hair, blue eyes and white faces. They look really good and are very well dressed. But have you seen a single poor person at the stadium? There aren't any. The players are the only ones who look poor and they had the right to enter the stadium.

"My son cried and cried and I told him 'Where can I get you 200 pounds? Your father would have to be Mubarak himself to get you a ticket.' That's why you'll find me a little unenthusiastic about this championship.

"I want to tell you that's something that's never happened before. The spectators were always the poor. The second and third class seats were reserved for us. But now the only right we have is to lick the dust the rich walk on. And by the way, it's not just this tournament, because the World Cup isn't on television unless you pay. Pay and watch. It looks like we're banned from seeing or watching anything. That might work in a country like Saudi Arabia or the Emirates, but here, how can we pay?"

Twenty-six

"Sixth of October City, Sixth of October, Sixth of October!" I was shouting out to persuade some taxi to stop but it was impossible, not a hope. I had an appointment at Media Production City at 10 o'clock in the evening and my car had broken down and I imagined I would find a taxi easily.

But all things come to he who is patient. A taxi stopped and the driver examined me closely before telling me to jump in. I jumped in.

"So what's the story?" I asked. "I've been here half an hour and no one wanted to stop for me."

"No one's going to stop for you," the driver said.

"Why, for heaven's sake?"

"At night and in isolated places and in Sixth of October in particular it's hard these days."

"Why? What's the problem?" I asked.

"There've been some incidents," he said.

"Goodness gracious. What happened, God preserve us?"

"There've been customers taking taxis and asking to go to Sixth of October and in some remote spot they take out flick knives and take all the driver's money and leave him on the side of the road and steal the car. One driver resisted the other day and they cut him to pieces."

"They killed him?" I said.

"No, he didn't die, but they stabbed him about 20 times all over his body. He was between life and death. He was destined to live a second life. The big problem is he'd just bought the car and of course it wasn't insured, and they stole it, those sons of a bitches. They'll cut it up and sell it as spare parts."

"How did you hear this? Was it published in the papers?"

"No, I don't read the papers. I can hardly afford to eat, let alone buy newspapers. No, I'm from Embaba and I was sitting at the coffee shop and I came across some drivers who had a piece of paper with these incidents written on it. They were giving it out to all the drivers and they gave me several copies for me to give out as well to the drivers I know. That's why I had a good look at you before I let you get in. I'll take you there and go straight home. Ever since then I haven't liked to stay out beyond 10 o'clock. The country's no longer safe. Ten o'clock at the latest I go and sit with my wife and kids. I'll drop you off and lock up the car and go straight to Embaba and may the Lord save us."

The story frightened me, but I liked the idea of the drivers sticking together and distributing a warning flyer.

I got out at Media Production City and I noticed that for the first time I was looking to the right and to the left.

Twenty-seven

I put my 14-year-old daughter May in a taxi in Agouza to go
to the Gazira Club, a short distance, which hardly takes two
minutes. It was the first time in her life she had embarked on
the adventure of going to the club alone. I had encouraged her
to do it because she's on the athletics team as a sprinter,
doing the 100 metres, the 200 metres and the 4 x 100 metres
relay, and she has to go to the club every day for training.

The day before, we had sat down together and I started
to talk to her about the need for her to take on the world,
because her permanent attachment to us was a stage to be
followed by another stage where she would rely on herself.
I said this would give her self-confidence, and she mustn't
be frightened of taking a taxi alone, because the Egyptians
are the kindest people in the world and when the driver
finds a young girl he treats her as though he were her
father.

The next day my daughter really did take a taxi alone and
the driver was a man in his 40s. As soon as they had gone up
the ramp on to the Sixth of October bridge he started his
questions:

"So do you watch porn movies in French or English?" he said.

May tried to think how to answer but she drew a blank so she held her tongue.

"Don't be frightened of me," the driver continued. "Seriously, tell me which language you watch porn in. I mean, do you like to hear the moans in English or in French?"

The poor girl was terrified and I don't know for sure what went on in her mind in those dreadful moments. She had arrived and she threw the money on the seat and took flight.

When my daughter told me the story, I recalled the wonderful film *Dreams* by Akiro Kurosawa, when the mother shuts the door of the house in the face of her child and gives him a dagger to take on society. Kurosawa filmed the scene beautifully as he walks away through a field of flowers, magnificent but deceptive at the same time.

This driver has lifted from my eyes the veil of illusion and I'm standing now in the kitchen sharpening the knife to give to my daughter tomorrow morning.

Twenty-eight

The question of the Capital Taxi project preoccupied many drivers and many conversations dealt with the idea, which was proposed during the time of Prime Minister Ahmed Nazif's first cabinet and relaunched with his second. Years have passed and the project has only just seen the light of day, though now they have dubbed it the Cairo International Taxi. What does 'international' mean here? Why international? Is it the taxi that's international or is it Cairo, and has the city been internationalised? It's incomprehensible, and if you could understand it you would have a fit of anger, or pangs of sympathy, depending on your point of view. The taxis will be yellow like New York cabs and will have the word CAB written on them in English to give them an international flavour. The drivers of the old black-and-white taxis, the ugly ducklings, kept seeking out every detail of the preparations for the yellow cabs – the cygnets – and the system of fares. They wondered who would take these taxis, and would this project affect them.

"Have you heard?" I said. "They're finally going to launch the Capital Taxi this month and they're going to cut into some of your business."

"They've been talking about that project as though it's the project of the century for the whole country. They're done with Toshka and now they've started on the Capital Taxi. Old man Nazif can't talk about anything else, it's become his favourite topic. They have cabinet meetings about it, and tea and coffee and soft drinks about it. They're going to great trouble and I don't know why. They say they'll start out with 150 cars and they'll increase it until there are 1,500 cars, while in Cairo, which is still the capital, there are already 80,000 taxis. Where will they be visible? That's like putting a grain of sugar in the water of the Nile. It reminds me of the story of the Lebanese president who went to China and the Chinese president said: 'Why didn't you bring the Lebanese people with you?' Because they wouldn't have been visible there.

"At first I was anxious but then months passed and years and the government as usual couldn't do anything. Then when I heard the numbers and the prices I knew that it was only for show. Just to look good, like everything else in the country. The 'Smile for the Camera' routine.

"And then the Capital Taxi is exactly the same as the Limousine system that Jihan el-Sadat set up. It was for foreigners only, which all goes to show that the government only cares about tourists and the rich, and we pick up the poor people that the government wants nothing to do with.

"But the hilarious part is I heard the project kept getting delayed because of the radio issue, you know. The frequency, I mean. The cars are all meant to be linked together. The customer calls on the phone and on the radio they see which empty taxi is closest to the address. Then they call up the driver and tell him to go there.

"The police left the government to talk about it as though it were the project of the century. They left it until it was done and they had bought the cars and then they told them 'Stop. That frequency is ours and only for us.'

"Just like someone who lets you park and stands watching you and after you get out of the car, he tells you: 'You can't park there. Move it along a little.'

"That's what happened. After they'd finished work on the project, they jumped on them and said: 'It won't do.' It's national security and my aunt's security, in which case I suppose National would be my grandfather.

"Between you and me, I was delighted. Long live the police in the service of taxis. Let them go and stop their project.

"Anyway, that project can go either of two ways. Either it loses money and closes down, or it puts up its prices really high and then I don't know who would use it, other than international people."

Twenty-nine

The question of education and private lessons is right at the top of the list of Egyptians' concerns, in a place shared only by the struggle to make a living. The two questions dominate the thinking of the great mass of the people, since Egyptian society is fundamentally family-based and children fill the Egyptian family with clamour, love, hope and, definitely, worry about the problem of education and private lessons.

To complete the cosmic cycle, every Egyptian struggles to make a living so that he can give his earnings to private teachers. Private lessons are like brand names. You can find them at all prices to suit every class and segment of society. Maths lessons can be for 10 pounds a session, and equally for 100 pounds. If your income doesn't permit you to pay 10 pounds, then there are classes for revision, group lessons and study centres, businesses in every shape and form.

With a driver who has children of school age, you only have to push the education button for him to set off like a rocket and no one can stop him, not even Nasa engineers in person.

On that day in September 2005 I had paid the school fees of my three children and as soon as I sat down in the taxi, the money I had paid to the school still hot in the safe, I pressed the start button and off the driver went:

"My children are going to give me a stroke. My only boy's in the sixth grade primary and I swear he can't write his own name, but at the end of the year they help him cheat and he passes to the next year or else the school's in trouble and gets cross-examined by the ministry. I also have two girls in secondary school, one in the third grade and the other in the second grade secondary.

"Thankfully the girls are clever, but they cost me the earth in private lessons. I pay 120 pounds a month on each one. Imagine, each of them takes private lessons in three subjects and each subject costs 40 pounds a month, enough to drive us to ruin double quick. As for the boy Albert, when he grows up, dimwitted as he is, how much will I spend on him for private lessons?

"You know what we do? Evelyn, that's the elder girl, gives him private lessons and gets money from me to pay for her private lessons. Because I have to teach her to make her own money through her efforts."

He laughed.

"But it's clear she's useless and doesn't know how to teach anything. All she does is take money from me."

"Okay and what's with the school?" I asked.

"What do you mean school? I tell you he can't write his own name. You call that a school? That's what free education brings you. The veil of shame has finally been lifted. These days, if you don't pay anything you don't get anything. And the trouble is that we do pay anyway. In the primary school we pay 40 pounds to get the books and in middle school and secondary 80 pounds and 100 pounds. Unless you pay there are no books. I mean the system is, either pay or no books.

"Education for everyone, sir, was a wonderful dream and, like many dreams, it's gone, leaving only the illusion. On paper, education is like water and air, compulsory for everyone, but the reality is that rich people get educated and work and make money, while the poor don't get educated and don't get jobs and don't earn anything. They loaf around, and I can show them to you, they can't find anything to do, except of course the geniuses. And our boy Albert is definitely not one of those.

"But I am trying with him. I pay for private lessons like a dog. What else can I do? I say maybe God will breathe life into him and he'll turn out like Ahmed Zeweil who won the Nobel prize for chemistry."

Taxi

Thirty

I consider myself extremely hostile to intellectual property
rights, in light of the gap that grows every day, or rather
every moment, between the developed world and us in the
backward world, and because I believe that every path must
be opened for the nation to which I belong to have access to
the culture and the medicine it needs to confront the evil
twins – ignorance and disease – which have devastated my
society for centuries. That obviously will not come about
by protecting intellectual property rights, which will
make medicines affordable only for the rich and which will
make culture a luxury which maybe the rich themselves
cannot afford. As a consequence of all this, I was sitting in
a computer company having installed software on my
computer that was either copied or pirated, because the prices
of the original software qualify as a bad joke. After I'd
finished copying a large number of pirated programmes and
installing them on my computer, I left the company offices in
Kasr el-Ainy Street to look for a taxi. While I was standing on
the pavement, a shoeshine man came up to me. "Want a
shoeshine, sir?" he asked.

"I'm waiting for a taxi," I said.

"It's two o'clock in the afternoon so you won't find a taxi straight away. Have your shoes shined first and then I'll get you a taxi. Besides, look sir, your shoes are very dirty," said the shoeshine man.

"Go on then, clean them."

"Where are you going, sir?" he asked.

"I'm going to Zamalek."

"Could you take me with you, for the love of God?"

"No reason why not," I told him.

"God preserve you," he said. "Do you have any children?"

"Yes, I have three."

"Snap, I have three too, one in the second year of the Azhar institute, but unfortunately he's gone to Tanta in the Delta, one in the second grade at secondary school and the third of the brood is in the third year of middle school."

"You're slightly ahead of me, but you look young, you don't look old enough for that," I said.

"I'm 45 years old and I got married when I was 21. But, God be praised, Our Lord has helped me prosper and the kids are turning out splendidly. They're all diligent students and they come top of the class. What bothers me is that boy, whose marks meant he had to go to Tanta. But within the year he'll transfer to Cairo," said the shoeshine man.

He took out a photograph of himself and his three children together. It looked like a recent picture and they all had broad smiles. The father was standing in the middle with his arm round his eldest son, who was standing on his right, and his other arm round his daughter, who was standing on his left. The youngest of the three was standing in front of the father, and his brother and sister each rested a hand on the shoulder of their little brother.

"This is a picture my brother took for us," he said. "He's been living in Saudi Arabia for getting on 20 years."

"Lovely picture, God preserve you."

"God be praised, Our Lord is very pleased with me. Everything's perfect. The kids are growing up and flourishing. Does anyone in the world need more than that?" he said.

"Look, there's a taxi. Zamalek! Zamalek! Are you coming with me?"

"I'm coming, didn't we agree?"

"We agreed."

So we got in the taxi. I sat in the front next to the driver, and he sat at the back and put his shoeshine box on his lap. The driver looked at the shoeshine man in disgust and then addressed me:

"Are you together?" he asked.

"Yes, we're together," I said.

"What do you mean together? No. Each of you will have to pay a fare," said the driver.

"I told you we're together."

"Okay, I'll take seven pounds," he said.

"Okay, perhaps you might talk politely."

"That's the way I am, rude What's it to you?"

Suddenly the shoeshine man got out and I got out after him, but he ran into the stream of traffic. I called after him but there was no reply. He disappeared into the midst of the crowd. I looked angrily at the driver. "What are you? Aren't you a human being?" I said.

Strangely, the driver didn't answer. He drove off and I decided to walk the rest of the way to Zamalek. When I arrived, I found that my shoes were dirtier than they had been in the first place.

Thirty-one

When the distance is very short I don't try to start a conversation with the driver, and this time I had got in on Arabian Peninsula Street in Mohandiseen, bound for Lebanon Square, a journey which does not last three minutes.

The driver was listening to the song 'I Still Remember' by Umm Kalsoum, and this was another reason for me to hold my tongue and enjoy the song, for taxi drivers rarely play beautiful songs.

But this time the driver gave me no respite and asked me a very strange question: "Do you know what's the most horrible thing in the world, sir?"

At first I thought he was joking but I could see that his face was serious.

I thought a while and answered: "If Egypt had been beaten yesterday in the match with Ivory Coast?" This was the day after the final of the Africa Nations Cup, which ended in an Egyptian victory at home over Ivory Coast, through a penalty shootout.

"No," he answered. "There's something much more horrible."

"Like what?" I asked.

"That someone should fall in love with, excuse my language, a whore," he said.

"Do you know anyone who fell in love with a whore and told you about it?" I asked him.

"Me, sir," he said. "I'm in love with, excuse my language, a whore."

We had reached the Pasqua Café, where my sister and my cousin were waiting for me, but the driver had aroused the curiosity that lies within us like a burning fuse and, besides, he had a strong desire to tell his story.

The taxi stopped and I continued the conversation.

"How did that happen?" I asked.

"Once I stopped for a woman in a headscarf, very respectable looking, about 11 o'clock at night, and she asked me to take her to Mohandiseen. That was at the end of August, in other words about five or six months ago. I took her to Damascus Street and she told me to come back in two hours because she was visiting someone who was ill and she wouldn't be able to get home that late, and may God reward me. I'm originally from the south and I thought this is a woman and the night is treacherous, so I agreed with her that I would come back in two hours. So I went back and she came down and asked me to take her to Manshiet Nasser. I asked her for 25 pounds and she said she would go doubles and give me 50 because the customer was very generous.

"As soon as she said 'the customer', I felt the word hit my eardrum like a rocket and pierce my skull, and my face dropped.

"Amal, for Amal was her name, said: 'I mean, what did you expect me to tell you? I mean, honestly, does any woman go visit someone sick in the middle of the night? Shouldn't you be open-minded?'

"So we started chatting and I felt sorry for the girl and I agreed to take her the next day to the same address at 10 o'clock at night. To make a long story short, this went on for a week and after that she said: 'Thanks, if you need anything, here's my mobile number and give me a call.'

"I don't know what happened to me. I couldn't think of anything but that whore and I kept saying to myself 'prostitute, prostitute'. What made it worse was that whenever I was going down the street I would see her. I'd go and brake and find it's some other girl but the same height, or some other woman in a headscarf, or even nothing like her at all. I thought I'd gone mad and that the girl for sure had cast a spell on me, so I went and called her on the mobile (and asked to meet her???) and when I saw her I found myself telling her 'I love you'. Dunno how. She laughed out loud and said: 'Do you want to screw or do you want to play around?'

"I said I wanted to get married, and she said back: 'Then you really are an idiot'.

"And I don't know what to do, sir. Imagine, a guy from southern Egypt like me, from Sohag, in love, deeply in love with a whore. I think about her all day and all night. I see her image in every woman, I love her.

"God spare you such a thing, because it really is the greatest curse in the world."

I got out of the taxi and told him through the window: "That way you didn't screw, you didn't get to play around and you didn't get married, God help you."

Thirty-two

We almost collided with several cars within a few minutes of setting off, and every time divine intervention would save us from certain disaster. The driver was a reckless youth with a shaved head, thin almost to the point of invisibility, his clothes loose and ill-fitting, probably because his size was to be found only in children's shops. His face was pale from chronic malnutrition and he was short in stature. His physical and medical condition reminded me of the horrifying statistic that 10 per cent of the children in southern Egypt are mentally retarded from malnutrition, and similarly of the report I heard on Egyptian Radio, which said the Air Force has a problem finding new airforce pilots, because all the applicants, with very few exceptions, are rejected for reasons connected with their physical or psychological fitness, and the general in charge said that this undoubtedly reflected the widespread malnutrition in Egyptian society.

This wretched driver was an excellent example of this phenomenon. But this was not the time to think about public problems because it looked like I might die in an accident within minutes. I still don't know how we didn't run into another car. Thankfully we turned into a crowded street and came to a complete stop.

"Where did you learn to drive?" I asked.

"In the army," the driver replied. "I just graduated."

"Graduated from what?"

"From the army. I worked as a driver. I learnt to drive and worked as a driver. We were based on the Suez road and I used to drive big army trucks," he said.

"In the desert?" I asked.

"Yes, in the desert."

"I think you should make do with driving in the desert," I said. He didn't get the joke and he went on talking.

"The army, those were the best times. I spent three years there and I don't think I will ever have it so good, companionship and friendship, because now I have so many friends, real friends, I mean men you can find when you need them. Frankly everything I know now I learnt from the army, not just driving, no, everything. The army's a real school, a school that produces men. After my military service was over, I wanted to volunteer but then came the story of this taxi and that distracted me a little."

"You wanted to volunteer!"

"Yes. It was a wonderful life. Steady salary, and there's nothing better than a government job, even at the bottom of the ladder."

"And if you did volunteer and get your government job, how much would you make?"

"No, a very good salary. I mean, in the region of 350 pounds a month. Who else can earn that much? But, you know, the taxi distracted me a little."

"Do you make good money with the taxi?" I asked.

"I really don't know. What I earn I spend straight away."

"About how much, I mean?"

"I've never worked it out," the driver said. "I make a pound, spend a pound, make 10 pounds, spend 10 pounds. I'm fatalistic about it, and by the way there's not a single taxi driver in Egypt who can tell you how much he earns. It's all in the hands of God."

The traffic began to thin out gradually and I was worried about driving on with this driver. 'He who fears survives,' I said to myself. I got out of the taxi and began to look for another one.

Thirty-three

This driver was angry, in fact very angry. I might say that he was in a rage. He was shouting in my face as though I were the cause of all his problems.

He was a young man of about 30 and looked like he'd been to university. I tried in vain to calm him down and in the end he told me why he was angry.

"Yesterday they pulled my driving licence and what did the guy say? He said I was talking on the mobile. I swear I wasn't talking on the mobile, I was only holding it. I tried to get the licence back through a contact of mine but the check-point had gone. This morning I made a trek to the Nikla traffic department at the end of the world because we taxi drivers are scum and they have to throw the department which deals with us to the far end of the world of Islam, then the guy who handles the papers said the licence hadn't reached the department yet. They wasted two hours of my work time yesterday and two hours today, and still no licence. I've yet to see how much I'll pay and how low I'll have to stoop to get it back. Drives you crazy. And at the traffic department it's packed and at every step you have to cough up money and pay bribes, it's disgusting.

"I don't understand what they want from us. There are no jobs, then they tell us to do any job that's going but they're waiting in ambush for us whatever job we do. They plunder and steal and ask for bribes and where it all leads I don't know. Just as I spend so much a day on petrol, I have to put aside bribe money for the traffic department every day just in case.

"Well in the end we'll all give up and push off like everyone does. It's clear that's the government's real plan, to make us all push off abroad. But I don't understand who the government will rob if we all push off. There won't be anyone left to rob.

"I really don't understand what the interior minister, before he goes to sleep at night, thinks he's doing to us. Does he realise that we're educated, well brought-up people, and how much our parents suffered to educate us? Does he realise how much we're abused by his policemen on the street? When his head's on his pillow, does he realise that we're done for and we can't go on and we're going to explode? We really can't take it. We're killing ourselves to make a living, and the Interior Ministry treats us as criminals, and liars of course. We're all liars as far as any police officer is concerned. It's clear they teach them that at police college, that human beings are born liars, live as liars, breathe lies and die liars. When I told him yesterday that I wasn't talking on the mobile, he said: 'But look, you're holding it in your hand and you were talking.' He didn't think for a moment that I might be telling the truth. The truth! How could I tell the truth when we're all liars and we're bastards and we have to be beaten like old shoes. I really feel that we aren't human beings, we're old shoes.

"What do you think, sir, am I a human being or an old shoe?"

He looked at me expecting an answer, and I couldn't help laughing, because his rage was so intense that it called for laughter and perhaps tears too. Then I apologised and said: "A human being of course."

In the end he said: "One worry makes you laugh, another makes you weep."

He apologised for having vented his anger at me, explaining that I was the first customer he had picked up after coming back from the traffic department.

After he had calmed down a little, he said: "Do you know what's the reason for the whole problem?"

I asked the reason and he said with a laugh: "The story is that as I was driving along I got a text message and I looked down and found it was a joke, and I laughed out aloud as I was coming up to the checkpoint. They thought I was talking on the mobile. A joke caused me all this shit."

"And what was the joke?" I asked.

"We thank all those who voted yes in the referendum and we give special thanks to Umm Naima because she voted yes twice."

Together we burst out laughing.

Thirty-four

I was on my way to Heliopolis where I had an important appointment at the Armed Forces public relations department to get permission to film in front of the podium where President Anwar Sadat was assassinated back in 1981. The appointment had been arranged a long time before and I did not want to be late, so I went at least half an hour early.

I took a taxi from Dokki and we took the Sixth of October bridge. The traffic was heavy as usual but I was feeling smug about the way I'd planned it. By about the time I had expected to be there, we had reached Salah Salem Street, and as we approached the exhibition ground the traffic came to a complete standstill. I wasn't very worried but the waiting dragged on and the minutes passed slowly and we started to ask the cars nearby what the reason was. They told us that President Mubarak was making an excursion. Okay, I thought, may he arrive safely, and in a few more minutes the road would clear.

We stayed sitting in the car, which by some magical power had been transformed into a mere rock squatting in the middle of the road, unable to move a fraction of an inch, even if Hercules had been pushing. After we'd been waiting close to an hour, I decided to pay the driver the fare and get out and walk, for no doubt, I thought, walking would be better than sitting. As soon as I started to get out, a police officer approached me and prevented me from getting out.

"What do you mean?" I said.

"It's forbidden, sir," he said. "You have to stay in the car."

"What do you mean? This is a street and I want to walk in the street," I said.

"It's forbidden, sir. Get back in the car."

I got in the taxi dejectedly and the driver laughed. "You mean you wanted to leave me in this mess! See what God does," he said.

"I was trying to make my appointment," I said.

"Forget that. This is one big jam. Once I was stuck here for four hours without moving."

"Oh my God, four hours!"

"That day I got out of here, took the car back to the owner, paid him everything I had on me and told him 'Never mind, I'll give you the rest tomorrow'. I went home and by God we all went to bed without dinner. My wife and kids had been waiting for dinner, like, all day long, and I came home empty-handed. My wife cried and put the kids to bed. I stayed by the window listening to the Koran to calm down."

"So what are you going to do today?" I asked.

"That depends on you. You could compensate me for however many hours we get stranded here."

"So that whole story was so that I'll pay you for today?"

"No, I swear on the Holy Koran. What I'm telling you is the honest truth, and if you don't want to pay more than you've paid that's okay by me. But stay with me to pass the time of day."

We sat for three hours, passing the time of day. He told me how he once loved Cairo with a passion, then he began to like it, then he began to have conflicting feelings about it, then he disliked it and now he loathed it.

In the end he told me about 20 jokes and I told him just as many back. Unfortunately I can't tell you them because any one of them would be enough to send me to prison for slander, although I don't see why I should go to prison because of jokes which most Egyptians know and which they circulate and laugh at daily.

Since I naturally do not want to be jailed, suffice it to say that we laughed a lot, even if I did not make my appointment. Since then I'll never feel smug like that again.

Thirty-five

'This is Cairo, and here is the news.' Then the newsreader, of course after saying in detail what President Mubarak had done during the day, regaled us with countless incidents and explosions across the world, in Israel, Iraq, India, Pakistan and the Philippines.

"Why do they insist on thinking we are mentally retarded and drooling idiots who haven't left the nursery yet!" said the driver.

"Ever since I remember, whenever some disaster takes place, they bring us news of the same disasters from all over the world. If we have a train crash then suddenly for days we hear about every train accident that takes place anywhere in the world.

"When the plane crashed in Sharm el-Sheikh or was shot down, they told us about every plane accident in this world and the next world, even accidents with crop-sprayers.

"This time after the terrorist incident in Tahrir Square they've been rubbing our noses in incidents from all over the place. Yesterday I heard that someone was walking down the street in America and he shot some other guy in the street. As you can see, that's a major incident. Tomorrow they will tell us there have been terrorist operations in Cloud Cuckoo Land and in the country where they ride elephants.

"Then the woman who presents the children's programme comes on and lectures us on the radio in her drink-up-your-milk-before-you-go-to-bed voice and gives us advice in her sympathetic-mother voice as though people still haven't given up wearing their bibs.

"I'd like to know if perhaps someone once told the Minister of Information, this one and the one before him and the one before him, that we are mentally retarded, or maybe they told him we were still at our mother's breast.

"And then they don't give up. Every time it's the same story repeated, until you no longer want to listen to the radio or read the newspaper.

"Between you and me, we're also fed up with news about the President. Every news bulletin, it's the President met so-and-so or phoned so-and-so, or so-and-so called him on his mobile. What's it to me who he spoke to or what he went to open? But the news that matters to us, there's no mention of it. It's disgusting. Everyone who wants to kiss ass kisses ass at my expense. I think they should do bulletins with serious news and other bulletins which have bullshit news and call it that way, so that the President can listen to the bullshit bulletins and then promote the people who write them, while we listen to the rest of the bulletins.

"I'd really like to tell the Minister of Information that we're a thousand times cleverer than him and that we understand the world a hundred times better than him. But where would I see the Minister of Information for me to tell him. What do you say I send him a telegram? Or might they arrest me if I sent him a telegram? What do I care that this used to be our country? Now it's their country and they do what they like with it. I'd better just stick to the taxi."

Thirty-six

In the government newspapers today they published the pictures of the people who have applied to stand in the presidential elections, with a short biography of each of them.

"I tell you," said the driver, "I've never in my life laughed like I laughed today. When I saw the newspaper and the pictures of the candidates I laughed till I cried. They look like Ali Haksha and Sousou al-Aaraj. It's really enough to make you die laughing. They've brought people no one has ever heard anything of.

"You'd find that even their mothers haven't heard of them, not even that clown guy they keep blowing up till he's the size of a balloon so they can say that even Mr Balloon is standing in the elections.*

"Do you know why these people are in this game?"

"Why?" I asked.

"They say, and God alone knows the truth, that absolutely no one wanted to stand, because it's not a game for anyone other than the government. Why would they stand? The

---

* The driver mentioned a particular name but a lawyer friend of mine told me to leave it out for fear that he might sue me.

government wants to appear to the Americans as though it's democratic so that the aid money doesn't stop and the economy doesn't collapse, so they're putting on this show. Very well, but where will they find people to act in the play, because in the first place we don't have any actors of that kind to act in comedies. So they called in the big director, that's the guy who makes lots of television serials and understands these things. He said the government would give money for election advertising for every candidate, because the actors have to get their pay, I mean why only Yehia al-Fakharani?

"Several customers have told me figures but every one says something different. One of them told me the government will pay every candidate a million and another told me three quarters of a million. Of course they'll spend a quarter of that money on advertising and put the rest in their pockets and come home from the fair with some goodies.

"The big joke one guy told me and we had a good laugh about it – that one of the candidates standing against Mubarak to get his share of the pie said that he himself would nominate Mubarak. I really didn't believe him but the man swore to me that he really said that, because Adel Imam's no longer funny and he only acts for the Arabs, and people have stopped watching him, and Heneidi's films are useless, so they said 'Let's put on a show for the summer, to make people laugh instead of them sulking.'

"Did you see the pictures in the paper today, sir?"

"Yes, I saw them," I said.

"Didn't you laugh?"

"Honestly I didn't recognise a single one of them, and obviously that's ridiculous."

"Frankly I don't like Mubarak and normally I'd have said I'd be for anyone who stands against him in the elections, but after I saw the people standing against him I said no, Mubarak's still the best of them, I mean it's not a question of the best but he's the only one that anyone could vote for."

"So you'll go and vote for him?" I said.

"No, I don't vote for anyone, I mean of those who do go and stand."

Thirty-seven

Thirty-seven

Incidents of taxi drivers being cheated are common and I'll tell you two stories on the subject. The first I heard when I got in a taxi on the Nile corniche outside the television building, heading for Mounira. The quickest way was for us to cut through Garden City. The driver was trying to find another route but in the end he reluctantly agreed to my plan.

"Why? Do you have anything against Garden City?" I asked. "You prefer Zamalek?"

"Not really, I don't support any football team, not even Zamalek, and I don't care either way. It's just that I don't like going down that street," the driver said.

"Why?"

"Because I was conned there last month"

"How was that?"

"A very stylish man got in the taxi, looked like a real swell, very well dressed. He got in in Zamalek and told me to go to Maadi. I said fine and off we went. Then he said: 'If you don't mind I'd like to go into Garden City to get some medicine for my sister. Just a second and we can drive on to Maadi.' 'No problem,' I told him. We went into Garden City and stopped in front of a pharmacy. He got out and came back a minute later. 'We'll have to go back to Zamalek, or go to Maadi and come back quickly because I found that I don't have my wallet on me.' 'No problem,' I said, 'don't you live in Maadi?' 'Yes,' he said. So I said: 'I'll pay for the medicine for you now and when I drop you off in Maadi then you can pay me back.' The medicine turned out to cost 42 pounds and I gave him 50. He bought the medicine and came out of the pharmacy with a bag, and just down the road he had me stop in front of a building and said: 'One second and I'll be back.' I stayed there waiting about half an hour. Nothing. I went in to look for him. Nothing. I went to the pharmacy and told them what he looked like. The doctor told me: 'Yes, he bought some aspirin for 50 piastres and insisted on taking a bag so that he could remember the name of the pharmacy.'

"Ever since then I've hated coming down this street, because it reminds me of what an idiot I am."

As for the second story, it's a real classic and a large number of unfortunate drivers may have fallen for it lock, stock and barrel. But the driver who told me this story was a veteran with long experience of driving, not of criminality. He had been in the profession since 1966. In brief, the story is that a passenger asked to hire the taxi for half the day for 100 pounds. The driver accepted the offer, rather than spending the day driving round the streets. The driver drove him from one end of Cairo to the other and in the end he stopped in front of a building and asked the driver to wait for him five minutes. Of course the driver found out in the end that the building had another entrance.

That day and for the first time in many years, the driver cried at his stupidity and his wasted effort. He wasted the rest of the day looking for a relative to lend him the rental money he had to pay the owner of the taxi for his shift, which was 50 pounds. "The owner of the taxi I work on, is it his fault that I'm stupid?" he told me.

The veteran driver told me: "The world now is fish eat fish, big and small, all snatching and grabbing."

Want and poverty have turned humans into fish far and

wide. The stench of rotten fish fills my nostrils wherever I walk in Cairo. Now I have started to see fish turn wild in the ponds, in the swamps and in the drains that run along the roadsides, preparing to pounce on me at any moment.

Thirty-eight

I was in Safir Square in Heliopolis. One taxi passed by, then another and then I stopped the third. As soon as I was seated next to the driver he started questioning me on why I hadn't hailed the taxis that were right in front of him. I told him that I don't much like new cars like Suzukis and Hyundais because they are too small for my size. I prefer old cars like the Fiat 1400 or the Peugeot 504 and the like.

The driver was nostalgic about the old days, the days when a taxi was something precious, while now he drives round and round dozens of times before he can find a fare.

"It all began when they issued the decree that any old car can be converted into a taxi and then every Ahmed, Mahmoud and Mohammed went and turned his car into a taxi. Taxi driving became the trade of those with no trade, it was really a disaster."

"When did that happen?" I asked.

"That was in the mid '90s. Suddenly they opened it wide-open. Really, I know people who had cars fit for scrap and they turned them into taxis. And at exactly the same time in the mid '90s they set up a ministry of the environment and it started saying that the old cars were polluting the air and emitting tar, which went into the lungs. They sent people out on the streets to measure exhaust emissions and they gave us hell, and in the end they couldn't do anything about us.

"I mean one lot was going in one direction and in the other lot in a completely different direction, and the two of them were in the same government. How so? It doesn't make sense.

"Ever since then the streets have been packed with stacks of taxis. Know how many taxis there are in Cairo?"

"No, I don't."

"Today there are more than 80,000 taxis, too many of course. Can you tell me how we're supposed to make a living? For the life of me, I don't know."

"That decree really was strange, that any car could be turned into a taxi," I said.

"It's well-known, not strange at all. When they issued that decree what was going to happen?"

"What?"

"As we said, tons of cars were going to be turned into taxis. And there's business in it for the government and for lots of people. I mean, there's easy money for the traffic department. For every car to become a taxi you have to pay licence fees and so on to the traffic department and the new drivers for these taxis have to get commercial driving licences and there's plenty of money in that as well, and then all those taxis have to buy meters."

"Very well, and then?" I said.

"Some fat cat had imported a large number of meters and suddenly he'd cornered the market for all the meters in the country, and all the new taxis bought them from him. A meter cost more than 1,000 pounds on installment. It was a huge business. He made money hand over fist. One decree on a piece of paper and a tiny little signature, and one guy made millions.

"Then just a few years later they tell you there are too many taxis and they don't know why. They suggest withholding new licences or retiring old taxis or those in poor condition or they say we have to issue decrees banning taxis more than

10 years old, or other things we heard more than 10 years ago. It's dream talk because at the stroke of a pen they want to put tens of thousands out of work and send them home, since most of the taxis in the country are more than 10 years old. And where were they when they issued the decree on converting cars into taxis? They're the same people, they still haven't been changed.

"The trouble is that ever since then we can't find any passengers. People can't afford to ride in taxis. Nowadays the taxi passengers take the minibus, and we're left living off the Arabs from summer to summer, and those have gone too since the launch of Capital Cab which has come out for them. Frankly, the government does everything it can to turn us into beggars or criminals. You feel they're making a big effort to ruin us and our families, and don't forget that the taxi drivers in Cairo are no small number. There are about a quarter of a million of us. What they don't know is that they won't be able to do it because Our Lord is the one who provides livelihoods. He is the Provider and there is no Provider other than Him."

By this stage in the conversation the driver was in a highly emotional state. He put on a cassette tape and we started listening to a recitation of Koranic verses.

Taxi

Thirty-nine

I often take taxis with drivers who don't know the way very well and don't know the names of the streets. But this driver had the honour of not knowing any street at all, except of course the street he lived in. His absolute ignorance of Cairo astounded me, as though he were a blind man walking for the first time in a grand palace.

"What's up, man?" I said. "Aren't you a driver or what?"

"No, really sir, I'm not a driver," he said.

"So what do you do for a living?"

"I'm a smuggler."

"A smuggler!"

"What's wrong with that?" said the driver. "That was the last will and testament of my late mother. 'Son,' she told me, 'the way of the wicked is the way you can make a living in this country.' And anyway, I don't smuggle anything wrong and I don't do the country any harm. On the contrary, I do it good, I mean, it's something for one to be proud of."

"Are you having me on?" I asked.

"By the Holy Koran, I am a smuggler. What happened is that my father died and I came to bury him, and this is his

149

taxi that I'm working in until I work out what I'm going to do in life."

"And what do you smuggle, for God's sake?" I asked.

"I'm still a young boy and I've been working for a few years with a business woman in Salloum. With God's help we smuggle smokes from Egypt to Libya, I mean we buy honest to God in Egypt and sell honest to God in Libya. Didn't I tell you we benefit the country? You could call me a patriotic lad."

"What do you mean, smokes? Drugs, you mean?"

"Drugs? Do you honestly think you'd find someone in the drugs trade driving a taxi and working himself to exhaustion, and I'd tell you I'm a smuggler, just like that? Do you think I'm stupid or do you think I'm stupid? Smokes means cigarettes, packets of imported cigarettes."

"How does that work? What do you do?"

"It's a very simple business. There are several business women in Salloum who employ men under them and we're their apprentices. Our business is we buy the passports, if we're clever for 10 or 12 pounds, 15 at the most."

"What do you mean, you buy passports?"

"Because everyone has the right to buy six cartons of cigarettes from the duty-free shop. We make a deal with everyone coming out of Libya to buy the six cartons of cigarettes on his passport. The six cartons cost about 175 pounds, plus the 10 pounds for the guy with the passport, that makes 185. In one day we buy about 200 passports and then we smuggle the cigarettes into Libya. Because the Musaid customs post is easy, I mean people coming in cars get searched but if they find someone going across on foot then he can cross with no problem. We put the cartons of cigarettes in cloth bags and put them on our shoulders. After we smuggle them into Libya we sell them there for about 42 to 45 dinars, and the dinar then was worth four pounds 75, so one passport would bring in about 20 pounds profit. On the whole amount we'd come out with 4,000 pounds a day. That's the business, sir, an honest business."

"But I don't understand, aren't these cigarettes available in Libya?"

"These are particular imported brands from the duty-free shop and the Libyans love them. Should we tell them not to like them? I mean, it's all useful work."

"Do you smuggle only cigarettes?"

"No, sometimes we used to bring in a few videos and cassette players from Libya to Egypt from time to time. But the Salloum customs post isn't like the Musaid post. They are merciless. If they saw a bag walking along on its own, they would arrest it. But we still managed to cope, because I've been there for years. My father was a taxi driver all his life. He wanted me to drive his taxi, may he rest in peace. My mother said: 'Your father held us back and always gave us a wretched life. Son, go and find yourself some modern work, work that earns you some money. Can't you see how well all the people around us are doing? Travel. Go to Libya and maybe the Good Lord will give you a break.' But as I was on my way to Libya I found this work smuggling cigarettes. I thought my prayers had been answered and I used to send my mother everything I saved, thank God, I made her happy for a while until the good Lord remembered her. She was a real mother, may she rest in peace."

"So are you planning to hang out in Cairo driving your father's cab?" I asked.

"No way, sir. I saw with my own eyes, and no one need tell me, how my father lived all his life. I saw with my own eyes how he died without the money to pay for a shroud, and what's coming is worse than what's past. I'll work any honest job that brings in money, even as a gangster."

Forty

Forty

Place: Cairo International Book Fair at Nasr City
Date: 26 January 2005
Time: 2:15 pm
Temperature: Moderate
Event: A television programme about political participation, and conversations recorded with the general public (definitely not on air because live broadcasts would be a danger to the democratic climate)
Method: Between the conversations the interviewer gives the unfortunate public some lessons in good ethics for taking part nicely in politics. If necessary the interviewer uses barks and grimaces to keep people in their place.

As I was walking past the Ezbekia bookstalls, a man approached me and introduced himself. "I'm the production director of a television programme and we're filming here," he said. He asked if the interviewer could do an interview with me and assured me that my lady wife would respect me more highly once she saw me on television. And my children could tell their friends at school with great pride what happened to their father on the silver screen, or is it the bronze?

They fixed the microphone to my shirt and the cameraman put the camera in front of me. Behind him a group of small girls in full veils gathered next to the wall of the German pavilion, laughing at the sight of the film crew. The interviewer combed some of the few hairs left on his head and prepared to start filming. "Okay, one, two, three, rolling." The interviewer ambushed me with a question about the voting card and I told him this conversation I had with a taxi driver:

"Have you got your voting card?" I asked the driver.

"Oh my God, you want me to get a voting card? Those guys would monitor me and if I didn't vote for them they would arrest me and send me to Tokar prison."

I laughed. "What do you mean, monitor you? Are you kidding?" I said.

"I'm talking very seriously, 100 per cent. If I got a card they would monitor me and I would be registered with them and that would be a disaster. You're too naïve and you don't understand what's going on," the driver said.

Then I told the interviewer about my attempts to convince the driver that what he was saying was sheer madness and that this suspicion of the state, which is entrenched in our psyche, must be put to rest, but what I said blew away in the breeze. The driver didn't believe a word of it. On the contrary, he started to grow suspicious of me and I think in the end he was sure I was with the secret police.

I ended my interview on the television by saying this driver proved to me that talking about political participation in Egypt was a sick joke, a very sick joke.

I was hoping that my children could boast of me to their friends, or that my wife would have a touch more respect for me as soon as they saw me on the silver box. But it looks like I wasn't the right shape for them to fit me on the screen.

Forty-one

As soon as I got in the cab I discovered it was more like a cattle shed than a taxi. It smelt rotten, and filth surrounded me on every side. As for the dust, that was the least of it. When the taxi started moving I was surprised to find that every part of it was operating independently of all the other parts and that every piece had its own particular screech, creating a concerto that was extremely unpleasant.

I glanced at the driver and he didn't look much better than the taxi I was travelling in.

"What's this that you're driving?" I asked him.

"What can I do? The owner doesn't want to fix it. He doesn't give a damn. He'll keep running it like this till it conks out completely. (The driver was imitating the voice of the actor Mohamed Saad when he plays the character el-Lembi in that movie.) Anyway, if they brought me a cigarette kiosk with wheels on I'd operate it as a taxi. I'm a driver who isn't bothered."

"Okay then, mister, how much will you charge from here to Maadi?"

"Whatever you pay."

"No, let's agree first. You haven't driven more than a

couple of yards. 'Set the terms first and everyone will end up happy' as the saying goes."

"We're not going to disagree," said the driver.

"Well suppose we did disagree, we'd end up arguing in the street. So how much will you charge?"

"I don't want to lose out on my livelihood. What I earn comes from Our Lord and you are merely a conduit. Who am I to cut the flow?"

"Look, I'm the one who's going to pay. If you won't say how much you want, then you can drop me off."

"Suppose I told you I would charge you so much and you were planning to give me more. It's God who provides."

"When you go into a pharmacy and ask how much a medicine costs, does the pharmacist tell you 6.80, or does he say 'Whatever you'll pay?' You should be the first person to know how much the trip should cost."

"You mean you don't know?" he asked.

"I don't know."

"Well, what's it worth?"

"Fifteen pounds."

"Okay, make it 20," he said.

"Drop me off," I shouted.

"Okay done, 15 is fine. Agreed. (The driver grinned broadly.) Well you know what, I was going to tell you 10, and you said 15. That means if I'd done what you said I'd have done myself short. I tell you that so that you believe what's right is right. A driver shouldn't state his price. That way he leaves it to Our Lord."

"And if I had said 5?"

"No, impossible. Excuse me, but the trip to Maadi for five pounds?"

The car drove on, each part of it moving in a different direction, the various components playing the worst symphony in the history of mankind.

"Have you seen the film *el-Lembi*?" I asked him.

"No, I haven't seen it, believe me, but they say it's very good."

Only then did I realise that he wasn't imitating Mohamed Saad in the film. It was Mohamed Saad who was imitating him.

Forty-two

"You know, I have a big dream," the driver said. "A dream I live for, because without a dream you can't live. Otherwise you always feel sluggish and you can't get out of bed, you get depressed and start wanting to die. But someone with a dream you find sprightly and energetic, like a spinning top, a blazing fire that won't go out. I'll stay ablaze like that, going round and about and saving money for four years.

"You know what my dream is? To take my taxi in four years' time and drive as far as South Africa and see the World Cup there. I'll pile up the pennies for four years and then go explore the African continent from the north of it, where I am now, to the south of it. I'll cross every African country and drive up the Nile until I come to the start of it, as far as Lake Victoria I mean, and on the way I'll sleep in the car, and in the boot of the car I'll stack away food to last me two months, tins of beans and tuna, and a shitload of bread, because I really like bread.

"I'll look at the jungles and the lions and the tigers and the monkeys, the elephants and the gazelles. And I'll get to know new people, people from Sudan and all the countries beyond. I still don't know exactly which countries I will cross. I bought an atlas from the bookshop and looked at it but I haven't fixed the route yet.

"When I reach South Africa I'll go to the southernmost point on the African continent on the ocean and I'll look with my own eyes and see the South Pole from afar.

"Of course I'll go to all the matches. I'm planning to apply to the Football Federation here, which is next to Ahli Club in Zamalek, so they'll get me some tickets. Since we're all Africans together, they're bound to help us out.

"Basically I drive all day long. You know, I drive about 15 hours a day. I mean, I'm used to it. I'll have no problem driving to South Africa.

"That's my dream and I have to make it come true."

I didn't want to tell him that there's no paved road linking Abu Simbel, the last town in Egypt, with Sudan, and the road stemming from the Toshka road to Sudan is closed, and that there isn't even a continuous railway line linking Egypt and Sudan, or that even if he reached Sudan then he wouldn't be allowed to go to southern Sudan without security permits from the Khartoum authorities, which he would be not able to obtain. Or that Cairo taxis aren't allowed to leave the country.

I forgot to tell him that the African continent is fragmented and disconnected, completely colonised, and that the only people who can still travel there are definitely not the indigenous Africans but rather the white lords, who make the African doors which swing open only for them. Long gone are the days of Ali Baba, who could open doors just by saying 'Sesame'.

Forty-three

I was in University Lecturers' City in Saft el-Laban, right behind Cairo University, beyond the railway tracks. The place is a perfect example of Egypt's urban planning, for Saft el-Laban is a village which borders on farmland and, because of the brutal expansion of Cairo, high-rise buildings made of breeze block have parachuted in on the unfortunate village, imports from the cities and the embodiment of disgusting architecture. People from outside have descended on the village and the university lecturers' compound has also landed there from Venus, surrounded by a large wall to prevent the earthlings from entering.

While I was leaving this 'city' (and of course 'city' here means no more than a collection of a few apartment blocks inhabited by people from Venus) towards Saft el-Laban, and after carefully examining the architecture and the inhabitants I realised the extent of the disaster. The place was a real monstrosity of an indeterminate nature. A beautiful woman walked past me wearing a long rustic dress and earrings hanging from her ears. She was headed away from the city, her feet leading her towards a market place that was the dirtiest I have ever seen in my life.

From behind the market there began to appear legions of children coming out of school, a first wave of primary-school girls, all in Islamic headscarves, then a wave of boys all wearing uniforms of faded brown. They passed around me on every side as though I were a disembodied errant spirit, and I felt some tension, although usually the sight of children fills me with delight.

I caught sight of a taxi from the city and I ran towards it to escape, after besmirching my face in this salad bowl of humanity.

"Where would you like to go?" asked the driver.

"Anywhere. Just get me out of here!" I said.

"I'm going in the direction of the university."

"Then go," I said.

The driver did not set off as I had hoped, for the road was packed with dozens of minibuses without number plates, driven by devils of the tarmac. On my right I saw a boy about four years old come up to a slightly older girl and take her hand for her to help him cross the crowded street. He seemed frightened and a part of his uniform was torn. She seemed confident that she could find a way safely through the vehicles with this boy.

I too felt safe and my tension at the chaos subsided.

"See how sweet the kids are?" I said.

"They sure are sweet, but their parents are mad," he said.

"What do you mean?"

"They're mad sending their children to school."

"What do you expect them to do with them?" I said.

"The kids go to school and don't learn a thing. The parents keep on coughing up for private lessons from the age of 10 upwards. In the end the parents are penniless and the kids don't find jobs. I mean, it's sheer stupidity.

"Then you find those kids filling the streets all day long as you can see, kids going to school, kids coming back from school, petrol and pollution, dirt and noise, for nothing.

"Me personally, and a few of my friends with me, we pulled our kids out of education after primary school, and we save their private lessons money for them. When the boy or the girl reaches 21, we'll give them all the money we would have given to the private tutors. I swear it's better for the kid to start his life with a little money in hand, rather than with some meaningless education, education that didn't teach them anything in the first place.

"Me personally, I say to everyone around me, don't send your kids to school, don't send your kids to school, like it was my only mission in life."

"But my parents," I said, "they spent everything they had on my education and they didn't leave me any money, and through my education I've been able to work and live."

"That was in the old days," said the driver. "That was in the '60s. Today the only motto is 'Get smart, make money', and for your information 90 per cent of people live off business, not from anything else.

"We'll leave our kids some money to open a small shop or a kiosk or as an advance payment on a taxi.

"Today there's no industrial training that's any use or any agricultural training that's any use or any business training. And don't forget that kids, poor things, expect the best and think that they are well and truly educated, when they don't even know how to read. The only thing they learn in school is the national anthem and what good does that do them?"

Forty-four

The jinn, spirits, angels and our brothers underground do exist, for they live in the consciousness of every Egyptian in one way or another. Talking about the jinn is definitely no joke, because they are part of our religion, our history and our folklore. In the end the jinn are embedded in our psyches in the same way as mashed bean paste is mixed with green vegetables in the blender. In spite of this strong admixture, the jinn generally do not intrude on our daily lives, other than in instances that our feeble intellects cannot readily understand. When they decide to appear, then the outcome is as unfortunate as it was for the taxi driver who took me to the Sultan Hassan mosque and who asked me to pray for him in the mosque. Then he told me his story:

"Why don't you believe me?" he said. "Yet you believe what they say at school, or on the radio and on television. But you shouldn't believe that. Believe what ordinary people say. The jinn exist and live with us. My rotten luck is that I live in the flat I was married in. This is something we've seen confirmed a hundred times if we've seen it once. We've tried to frighten them away in every possible way but it's no use. As for us leaving the flat and moving to another one, that would cost a packet, no less than 4,000 pounds, of which I have about four pounds.

"A week ago my wife said to me 'Look, man, at the beginning of next month, if you don't find an answer to this disaster that has struck us, I'm up and out of this haunted house'. Well, how can I find a solution? And the bitch knows that full well."

"How did you find out that the house is haunted?" I asked.

"What do you mean how did we find out? It's as clear as the sun at noon."

"I don't understand. Please explain," I said.

"The first thing is when we wake up in the morning we find drawings on the wall, the same colour as the wall, but there's a damp line that's made the drawing. Lots of drawings but mostly eyes, big eyes and small eyes. Then at the end of the day the drawings disappear. The second thing is the house is full of geckos. Do what you can, you find geckos everywhere, geckos of every shape and colour, and colours, I tell you, that you've never seen before. Last night, for example, I saw a large gecko which was dark purple. Have you ever seen purple geckos? Lots of things. I mean, the strangest thing is the story of the female animals, no females will stay in the house."

"What do you mean?" I said.

"We keep birds. We put two male birds and two females together. We wake up in the morning and find the two females have escaped from the cage. How did they open the cage? How did they fly away? We don't know. Well, if the cage opened, why didn't the males fly away too? It's inexplicable and again it hasn't happened once, no, more than once.

"Then we brought in one of those women who understands the supernatural. As soon as she came into the flat, she said the house is haunted. We hadn't given her any idea. She knew straight away that there were jinn living in the house. Then what made matters worse with my wife is the woman said she wasn't having any children because of this problem and as long as we live in this house we won't have any children at all.

That was a month ago and ever since then my wife hasn't wanted me to come near her. She says to me 'What's the use, big boy?' And she's sworn an oath I won't touch her until we leave this haunted dump we're living in."

"So the old woman didn't say why the jinn are living with you in the house?" I asked.

"Oh yes, she did. She said the house was the jinn's in the first place and they wouldn't leave, even if you went in banging drums. She even refused to take any money and she didn't even drink her tea. She told my wife 'Go and cut your nails because the jinn come out of them. Then she whispered something in my wife's ear and for the life of me she adamantly refuses to tell me what she told her."

"That's amazing" I said.

"All this I'm telling you and you wouldn't believe me. I tell you, we go to sleep and wake up with pictures of big eyes drawn on the wall. Who's drawing them then? Is it my mother who's drawing them? The jinn exist. Don't let education mess up your mind, and thank God that your house isn't haunted."

"Thank God," I said.

Forty-five

About an hour before Friday prayers the streets of Cairo are almost empty. At that splendid time I was heading to Rihab City to visit a friend and the taxi driver chose to go via Salah Salem Street by way of Abdin Square. At the corner of the square a football suddenly flew in front of the taxi and out of nowhere sprang a young man running behind it, looking at nothing but the ball. We hit him and the jolt threw the young man at least three yards. When he landed he set off after the ball again, as though nothing had happened.

I asked the driver to stop to make sure the young man was okay but the driver refused and kept on driving at speed.

"We should have taken him to hospital. It may be that right now he can't feel what happened to him," I said.

"You mean if something had happened to him he would have run off like a deer in flight like that? It was a light blow and Our Lord kept him safe. Besides, if we went to the hospital it would be a whole palaver and we would never finish. Those people at the hospital would jump at the chance to act the bleeding heart, when in fact they're the ones who give us hell at every turn. As far as they're concerned, humans aren't worth anything, not even a cent. Didn't you see what happened with the ferry that sank in the Red Sea? People died in droves and the government stood there cheering. Much ado about nothing, pardon the expression. Do you know what I say human beings are like in the eyes of the government?"

"No," I said.

"Human beings in Egypt are like dust in a cracked cup. The cup can easily break and the dust will blow away in the wind. We cannot gather it together again and in fact there's no need to gather it together, because it's a just a little dust that's flown away. Human beings in this country are flying dust, with no value.

"You know the people who died on the ferry, for many of them they still can't get death certificates issued, because their official papers went down with them, poor things, a total mess. It's a crying shame, this country. Even the money they said they would give them, many of them haven't received any of it. They said they would get 66,000 pounds for a dead person and then there were donations from all over, from the Gulf and from businessmen, which would work out at not less than 50,000 pounds. Where's that money gone? No one knows. And the families, poor things, their sons are gone and they can't even get the money, and the owner of the ferry of course fled abroad as usual.

"Did you know too that 24 members of the ferry crew ran off and no one can find a trace of them. They say the owner of the ferry smuggled them off so they don't tell secrets that would get him in trouble, and so the insurance company will pay the money. Because if those people admitted to what happened, the insurance company wouldn't pay anything. Lots of disasters. And I heard a rumour, God alone knows, I don't much like to say 'God alone knows', but I heard this from people and I don't know where the truth is and where the untruth."

"What did you hear?" I asked.

"That the ferry was carrying 500 passengers extra beyond its capacity, but no one wants to say it. Of course the people who ran away know all these things," he said.

"Where did you get this information from?" I asked.

"It's just one of the guys in my hometown lost his son, poor guy, in this accident. His son was a building worker in Saudi Arabia and the father's at his wit's end between Safaga and here, and he told us what happened in Safaga. It was chaotic and brutal and heartbreaking. No one's got rights in this country.

"In the end the guy didn't get anywhere, and he keeps suing the government and the ferry owner, and the whole world.

"And then, have a look at who died on the ferry. The toiling workers who go to Saudi Arabia to be abused and have to sweat blood to make a pittance. The plane's too expensive for them so they think they'll save money by taking the ferry. In other words, just a few wretched workers, because these days disasters happen only to the poor. They pick them off one by one, and our turn will come in the end. And after all that, you want me to go to the hospital of my own free will?"

Forty-six

"Have you heard the story about the Ittihad football players?" asked the driver

"Which Ittihad?".

"Why, the Alexandria Ittihad. Is there any other one?" he said.

"Ittihad was travelling to play a match in some African championship and at the airport they discovered that one of the players had a forged passport and they arrested him. The rest of the team left on the plane. Now I've been listening to the news for 40 years and I've never heard of a player forging a whole passport. A visa or a stamp maybe, but a whole passport, that's amazing.

"And a few days ago there was the story of the singer called Tamer Hosni who forged his military service certificate to get a passport issued, and straight after that the singer called Haitham, he also forged an army certificate so that he could leave the country. They actually got their passports with the forged certificates, but Tamer has a bigger problem."

"Why's that?" I asked.

"Because they discovered in his papers that he'd forged a university certificate as well. A man who looks professional and the trouble is that he's a big star and his films are a big hit. Did you ever hear that Mohamed Fawzi or Abdel Halim forged passports? And the guy who's going to defend them? The guy who was in charge of Zamalek Club.

"Then there's that singer Shireen who forged her identity card to say she was unmarried when she was divorced, and lots of other cases. Forgery in Egypt is now as common as drinking tea, and there's even more that doesn't come to light. I had one passenger told me that many actresses change their date of birth so when they marry Gulf Arabs or Saudis they look like spring chickens. That's one way forgery can earn you riyals straight away, in other words legal prostitution with contracts registered. Do you know where the problem came from?

"Where from?" I asked.

"The problem started when everyone with two pennies to his name thought he could do anything with his money. Respect for the state is gone. With money I can drag the government's nose to the ground. I can forge a passport, change the entries on an identity card, anything. If my driving licence is confiscated, with money I can have it delivered to my house immediately.

"Everything's spread out on the pavement and offered for sale. Whenever someone gets in trouble you find he's fled abroad. How? With money. This month Mamdouh Ismail fled the country, Ihab Talaat's fled, and others. No need to talk about the months before that, or before that.

"And then they go teach the kids in school that values are more important than money and they make them memorise poems about principles, and that money comes and goes but morals are the pillars of a nation and the basis of humanity. Talk that goes in one ear and comes out the other. Don't they see what's going on around them?

"My daughter's still young, 16 years old, and in our day that was the age for love and romance, and we used to sit listening to Umm Kalsoum. But the bitch tells me 'What's that crap about love? I want to marry someone rich. It doesn't matter whether I love him or not. What matters is that he's rich.' I tell her there's nothing more wonderful than love in this world. It's love that keeps us alive, it's the air we breathe and it's what makes me put up with your mother. She tells me: 'In this world there's nothing nicer than money.'"

Forty-seven

Forty-seven

When I got into the taxi I was surprised to find the man sitting in front of me next to the driver was silently weeping. He was a brown-skinned giant with a bushy moustache. The calm was as thick as his moustache, and the night was in its last hours. The only sound was the intermittent and irregular breathing of the giant as he wept.

In our society it is a rare enough occurrence to see a man crying. To see a giant from southern Egypt crying is something you could put in the Guinness Book of Records.

The silence continued for some time, then the two men resumed their conversation, conveying to me a state of tension, the vibes between them highly charged.

The voice of the giant was breaking, and the driver's voice was full of grief. The whole conversation between them was doleful. The story gradually began to come together in my mind like the pieces of a puzzle, and the full picture did not take shape until I had arrived home.

The giant was a taxi driver from Alexandria who had come that day to see his brother, also a driver, to borrow some money. But you can't squeeze blood from a stone, as his fatalistic brother kept telling him.

The giant had had three operations on his spine in recent years after a long history of driving taxis, and the last operation was four months ago. His doctor had told him not to drive or else something with unfortunate consequences might happen to him. In the last four months the giant had sold everything he possessed and borrowed from everyone around him to get out of hospital and embark on a long course of physiotherapy. He explained in detail his unbearable backache but his dignity did not allow him to cry out in pain, especially in front of his wife and children. When all means of subsistence had dried up, his wife had had to work as a servant for a retired dancer more miserly than Père Grandet in Balzac's novel *Eugénie Grandet*, after he had sworn by everything holy that she could not work as long as he was alive.

Today he had to cover a cheque for 1,000 pounds that he had borrowed before the operation and if he did not pay it back then prison doors loomed, and who else in the world could he resort to other than his brother?

His brother had had the same operation some time back but at least he was still working as a driver. The problem was that it would be easier for him to find the ghoul, the griffin and the trustworthy friend than to find the sum of 1,000 pounds. He had just started paying the installments on a fridge, the down-payment on which had devoured the advance he had been saving to renew his taxi driver's licence, and even if he sold his wife he could not come up with this amount.

It was a calm conversation between two brothers and it seemed to me that affection and bankruptcy had brought them closer together. It was a conversation so tragic it was melodramatic, almost to the level of an Indian film, and as I watched, all that was missing were Indian songs and dancing. A tearjerker from Amitabh Bachchan would not have been out of place.

Throughout the conversation they were not aware of my presence, as though I did not exist or perhaps was wearing a cloak that made me invisible. Even when I got out and paid the fare, neither of them paid me any attention or addressed a word to me.

The two were praying, each whispering to the other, both turning their faces to the heavens on the chance that a portal would open there and their prayers would reach the One who Listens and Answers.

Forty-eight

The First Song
"I'm like a fish and the taxi's like a fish tank," the driver said. "The fish goes back and forth and the fish tank is a little prison. It bumps into the taxi window on this side and then it bumps into the window on the other side.

"I too stretch out my arms and bump into the window on this side, and I stretch out my other arm and bump into the window on the other side. It's true I drive around all day long but all I see is the inside of the taxi, my limits are the windows of the taxi.

"Life imprisonment, ending in the grave."

The Second Song
"My back's stiff from all the sitting. When I come to stretch out at night, I can't. My back hurts when I stretch it. And the taxi is old and has holes all over and the heat of the engine comes through on to my legs and my body in the summer. I'm like the kebab guy in front of his charcoal grill. The difference is that he smells the sweet smell of meat while I smell exhaust fumes."

Forty-nine

I was in Ataba on my way to the Pyramids. I thought I'd ride the metro to Giza and then take a taxi to the Pyramids. The weather was very hot and it was July, and I had been browsing in the Ezbekia bookshops (what used to be called the Ezbekia Wall), bookshop by bookshop to buy a book about crafts in Pharaonic Egypt as a present for my wife, but I couldn't find it. I went down into the metro station and came across a large sign reading: 'The Metro Underground: Mubarak's Gift to His People.' It really is a nice present. Here I was coming to Ezbekia to save a few pennies, and I wondered how much Mubarak paid for this metro. And in which market in France did he find it to buy it and bring it for his people?

It's infuriating. All year long the government has been talking about pluralism and democracy and the first multi-candidate presidential elections, and at the same time some unknown person writes in the metro that the president owns the state's property and uses it to buy presents for a group attached to His Excellency and called His People. Contradictions enough to give you apoplexy. We have to swallow stupidity pills to take everything that they tell us.

This sign really irritated me, especially as the day before I had seen another sign reading: 'Yes, O Noble Mubarak, Yes, O Lord, Yes, O Noble One, Yes Mohammed, Yes Hosni, Yes Mubarak, You Who Have the Support of God the Lord of the Universe and of Our Lord Muhammad, May God Pray for Him and Grant Him Peace, O Purest Son of the Offspring of Your Ancestors Ali bin Abi Talib, Fatima the Radiant the Virgin and Our Master Hussein, and so on...' We have descended into nonsense.

I got off the metro in Giza and took a taxi. There were banners around us on every side saying 'Yes' to the referendum for us to change the constitution to make it more pluralist, but at the same time: 'Yes to Mubarak'. The people were really confused. They felt they couldn't just say yes to changing the constitution. They were afraid, poor things, that maybe they had to say yes to Mubarak too. We drove on and I saw a banner reading: 'The baby in its mother's womb...says 'Yes to Mubarak'.

"What do you think of all these banners?" I asked.

"No, the nicest one I've seen said: 'A unanimous yes to Mohamed Hosni Mubarak and Mubarak's son and the son of Mubarak's son,'" he said.

"So it's a republican monarchy with hummus. What do you think?"

"What does Mubarak have to do with these banners? It's the fault of people who put them up. Frankly my view is that Mubarak's not to blame. The man's doing everything he can. He deserves his job. And besides, who would agree to take part in elections against a few people who aren't worth a piastre? He's been president of the republic for coming on a quarter century, and before that he was vice-president. I mean, he's a guy who fully understands the job, tried and tested and up to the position. For the sake of democracy he agrees to run in elections against people who have no experience. My God, no one would do that. I mean, Sadat for example, would he have agreed to do that? Impossible. And who thought up this idea? It was Hosni Mubarak as well. You know where that man's greatness comes from?"

"From where?" I asked.

"Because he's originally a pilot. A pilot has to be smart and alert all the time and very focused. If he nods off for a moment, it's instant death. There's no room for error. That's why Mubarak is 100 per cent. Focused all the time and he understands what he wants to do. It's enough what he's done in Cairo – with flyovers, tunnels and so on. It's amazing. You know in the '80s the streets were more crowded than they are now, and look how the number of cars has grown since then. The man's done a great job, and after all that he's agreed to run in elections with a bunch of nobodies. By God, he's good for us."

"But I was irritated with him today when I saw a sign in the metro saying that the metro was Mubarak's gift to his people," I said.

"So what's wrong with that?" said the driver. "The metro was Mubarak's idea anyway and it solved a massive transport problem for people. Did you know that more than a million people ride the metro every day. Didn't I tell you there's no one to match Mubarak? Now where did you say you were going?"

Fifty

"In a hurry?" the driver asked me. "I have to fill up with gas."
I said I wasn't, but I wasn't at all expecting the endless queue
of cars waiting at the station to fill up on natural gas. There
wasn't a single private car in the line, only taxis of every shape
and form. The queue stretched back like a black-and-white
striped snake starting at the gas station and ending with us in
the street, at least 50 yards away from the station. You could
safely describe the speed at which the line was moving as slow.

"What's the story with the gas?" I asked.

"Gas is much cheaper than petrol," said the driver. "It
works out at about half the price. For us as taxi drivers it's a
major saving. We drive at least 150 kilometres a day and a
Peugeot 504 like mine burns lots of petrol. It makes a big
difference for me."

"But I heard that it costs thousands of pounds to install," I
said.

"No, it's all done on instalments. Whenever you fill up you
pay a small extra sum until you find you've paid off the whole
amount. Personally I bought the system secondhand from
another taxi. The owner was going off to work in the Emirates
and he sold it to me for 900 pounds cash."

The queue hadn't moved much and we found the drivers gathered to the side of the station, leaving their taxis in the line and waiting for others to fill up in the station so they could move up in the queue. We got out, the driver and I, to join the other drivers, who were in a state of incessant collective laughter.

"They found tons of Viagra at the port in a consignment of ceramics. The advert on the radio tomorrow is: 'Ceramics with Viagra, so that women can make their men lick the tiles'," one of the drivers said.

Everyone roared with laughter and another driver quickly chipped in:

"Dosage for using Viagra: With a girl you're seeing for the first time, no need. With the woman you love, half a pill. With your girlfriend, one pill. With your wife, six pills, 10 beers and three whiskys, two joints of hashish, one of grass and God help you. It may work or it may not."

The roars of laughter rose to the heavens and one of the drivers quickly jumped in, before anyone else had a chance. "There was a guy from Upper Egypt whose father dies. He went and took some Viagra and they said: 'What are you doing that for, you madman?' 'In these difficult times,' the man said, 'I need someone to stand up for me.'"

Another driver spoke. "A taxi driver was fed up with his wife, so he put an ad saying: 'For exchange, one wife in good condition, factory-made interior, electric fenders, tubeless thighs, done 10,000, on blocks five years."

The driver laughed so much he collapsed on the ground. Another jumped on top of him, grabbed his hair and shouted in his face: "Pull yourself together!" Then they stood up, both laughing, and a group of drivers walked away to move their cars up the line towards the station.

Then a new round of jokes began.

"Know what's the best present you can get your wife? A ticket on the Salam ferry," one of them said.

"Okay, you know the theory of marriage?" said another. "Before the wedding, you speak and she listens. After the wedding, she speaks and you listen. After three years of marriage, you both speak and everyone else listens."

Hysterical laughter broke out and a new batch of drivers joined us, leaving their taxis in the queue. One of them started to tell a joke: "Here's the news 100 years from now: 'Hossam Hassan will receive the Africa Nations Cup from President Luay Haitham Gamal Mubarak, and the condition of former Israeli Prime Minister Ariel Sharon is improving.'"

Everyone guffawed and our turn came to move the taxi forward to fill up. As we were walking to the car, I heard one of the drivers say: "Listen to this very Egyptian joke. There was a monkey in the jungle and it saw some tigers running and a donkey running behind them. The monkey asked the donkey: 'Why are you running?' and it said: 'They say they're going to arrest the tigers.' So the monkey asked him: 'What's that to do with you?' 'It'll take me ages to prove I'm not a tiger.'"

I laughed wholeheartedly and thanked the driver for this break, because I hadn't taken part in such a collective laughter session for a long time, a very long time.

I decided that whenever I was at a loss as to what to do, I would come to this station and share some laughs with the taxi drivers – loud raucous laughs, laughs from the belly and definitely not from the heart.

Fifty-one

"So what are we going to eat?" the driver said. "Meat's too expensive, and not just expensive but it's got foot and mouth disease. Fish is doubly expensive. It was chicken we used to live on and cook with the broth of it. Frankly I don't know what we're going to eat."

"They say cook the chicken well and the bird flu virus dies," I suggested.

"You only have one life!" said the driver. "So the virus will die and what's to guarantee I don't too? Because you can't imagine what happened where we live. It was a disaster. I live in Sign Youssef near Sakkara and we were the first area in all of Egypt attacked by bird flu before the big scare. We have several poultry farms around us and thousands of them died. We got in touch with the government and it seems they hadn't prepared themselves yet so they told us: 'We can't do anything for you, go burn them.' And that's exactly what happened."

"You burned them?" I asked.

"Of course the idiots around us, instead of burning them or burying them, they went and took the dead chickens and threw them in the irrigation canal. Stupidity like I've never seen before or after. But that's what happened. They said: 'Are we really going to burn them? Are we really going to dig trenches and bury them? No, that would be too much trouble.'

"After that the stories started about the water being polluted and if we drank it we would die of flu. You know what this country's like for rumours and how timid people are, and I the first of them, of course.

"And wherever you walk down our way you'll find chicken feathers everywhere because when they came to throwing them the wind blew away the feathers. Then they said the feathers were dangerous, but thank God no one's caught bird flu in our neighbourhood."

"May God protect you," I said.

"So have you heard, if someone gets bird flu, what does he feel?"

"What?" I said.

"He feels like a chicken in front of his wife, and in the bedroom he'll feel that his wings have been clipped." The driver chuckled. "But the trouble is you feel like that even without bird flu," he added. "Honest to God!"

Fifty-two

Blah blah blah blah blah blah...

Then the driver looked back to have a good look at my face.

"You look like a decent type," he said.

"Thank you," I said.

"Everything I've told you was just bullshit, I'm afraid, but I'll speak to you frankly so you're in the picture with me. If I could, I'd kill you right now and take everything you have. I'd do it right away. If I was arrested, it wouldn't matter much to me, at least in prison I'd find someone to feed me."

I didn't know what to say.

"My God, I tell you, I'm living like a dead man. No, a dead man's much better off than me. I work two shifts and at the end of the month I'm still about 100 pounds in debt. I tell you, sir, a bull lives a thousand times better than us."

The driver was a young man of about 25 or a little less and he went on talking at high speed. "You know those kids who blew themselves up in al-Hussein and in Tahrir Square?" he said. "Those kids are top notch. Don't believe they're terrorists. They're a bunch of poor kids who saw where things are going, I mean, they saw things properly and they realised that death was much better than this son-of-a-bitch life we lead."

"Not to that extent!" I said, trying to calm him down.

"Not to that extent, it's all the same. You know, if suicide wasn't forbidden, everyone who knew them would have committed suicide ages ago. Those kids did something right. They wanted to kill two birds with one stone. They killed themselves and thought they would go to heaven as well. Nothing else matters. The story that they were part of an Islamist group and that there was a girlfriend involved, that's all lies."

After a short silence, the driver started shouting in my face. "Those were wretched kids, poor things, even the bomb they wouldn't know how to make it. It had a few nails you'd buy at the hardware shop for two or three pounds. What kind of group is that, that doesn't know how to make anything, poor things?" he said.

"No," I said. "They knew how, and they're wrecking the Egyptian economy."

The driver looked at me with disgust. "What economy?" he said. "We're famined (I assume he meant famished). We went broke ages ago. We've hit rock bottom. Besides, people don't do anything in this country other than steal from each other. That's the economy."

"I'm getting out of the right here," I said.

The driver stopped the car. "Don't you know how they made that nail bomb?" he continued. "Between you and me, I want to end it all at the next stop and go straight to heaven."

I hurried out of the taxi, to be slapped in the face by a hot blast of air from the polluted street.

Fifty-three

"Aren't you planning to stand for election after the change in the constitution and become president of the republic?" I asked the driver. "You must know half the people in the country from driving around all day long."

The driver laughed like a man weighed down by the burdens of humanity and of the more than 60 years which he must have lived, judging by the wrinkles on his face.

"So you're planning to vote for Hosni Mubarak?" I said.

"He doesn't like me. Why should I like him?" he answered, in all seriousness.

"Why doesn't he like you?" I asked.

He looked at me and asked: "Do you have a million pounds?"

"No," I answered, taken aback.

"Then he doesn't like you either. That man only likes people who have more than a million pounds."

"It's not a question of liking," I said. "You're not going to get married, you're going to choose the person who's best for the country."

"For me to vote for him, I have to like him, apart from the fact that I haven't voted in my life and I don't have a voting card, and I don't even know anyone who has a voting card. You know, after my long life, I've never seen anyone with a voting card. Do you have a voting card?"

"No," I said.

"What happens is a few village heads and the directors of government offices forcibly round up the peasants or the government workers to vote, to earn a little extra money. In the end it's a business. If you want the truth, the few people who blindly go and vote, not one of them is going of his own accord, except for a few millionaire thieves who do it for business."

"You seem a little pessimistic about the world," I remarked.

"I swear," he said angrily. "Out of the 70 million Egyptians, there's not one who votes willingly except, as we agreed, the millionaires."

"So you don't like the government?" I asked.

"Do you like the government?" he asked.

"To be honest, I think that Prime Minister Nazif is a man with very clean hands and we haven't had anyone with such clean hands in a long time," I said.

"He's a foreigner," the driver said.

"What do you mean by that?" I asked.

"He's Canadian, and he went to swear the oath there in Canada."

"I haven't heard that story," I said.

"Come on, how come you don't know that? He's Canadian, I tell you, Canadian. Hosni Mubarak chose a Canadian prime minister for us. After the elections which I hope Hosni Mubarak will win of course, he'll get us an American one called Johnnie Walker."

Fifty-four

I asked the driver to drive me to the television building at
Maspero. His face lit up as he asked if I worked in television.
When I told him that I didn't, he didn't give up.

"But you definitely know someone there?" he said.

"Oh yes," I answered.

"Because I urgently need to see Mufid Fawzi, the presenter,
very urgently," he said.

"Are you sure it's something really urgent?"

"This isn't something for me," the driver said. "It's for the
country. Because I want to tell him that every morning half
the passengers I pick up I take to the Cancer Institute. It's
very strange. As soon as I drop one off at the institute, I drive
around a bit and find another passenger going to the
institute. It's clear the whole country has cancer.

"I don't know if it's from the filth we have to breathe
in the street or the food we poison ourselves with, or
definitely from the pesticides we keep spraying, but what I
want to tell Mufid Fawzi is that every day about half the
Egyptian nation goes to the Cancer Institute, and he'll
definitely know how to handle it. He must know the
president and he's bound to talk with him about this

serious matter, and the president will definitely find a solution to this problem."

Fifty-five

"I see everyone who owns a private car as a criminal, a thief, no exaggeration I tell you, I look in their eyes and I see a bunch of criminals.

"See that poor girl who's standing there. Look at the car in front of us and what it'll do. See, it's pulled over and the guy's trying with the girl. Now he's gone off, rebuffed and humiliated. Didn't I tell you that everyone with a car in this country is a criminal, chasing after things which aren't theirs.

"See those kids standing there, they've come out of that secretarial institute on the right. See that car, my God, that's worth more than half a million pounds, he's parked like a dirty thief looking in the mirror and waiting for someone to approach him.

"It's despicable and disgusting. Whenever I'm driving, I see cars with nothing in mind but stealing. You know, a rich guy once told me: 'The rich fuck the poor every moment of their lives.' If you go work for a rich man he'll give you hell for three weeks and then he'll fire you and tell you you're no good, and he'll bring someone else and do the same thing to him. They fuck them.

"The trouble is they try to pick up girls aged 16 or 17, or the girls at that institute we saw, young girls, poor things, and pretty, who are trying to learn and make an honest living, and those guys are acting like wolves who want to get their teeth into their flesh, and the poor girls are still so innocent they don't understand the dirty minds of the criminals waiting in their cars.

"See that car too, that's got temporary import plates from Suez, see how big it is, big as a bus, he's parked there too, hanging around waiting to throw his dirt on to our street."

All along the way the driver continued to point out to me 'the thieves of the road', as he put it, and continued tirelessly to analyse the reason why each and every car was stopped by the side of the road. The strange thing is that I didn't utter a word throughout the journey, from the moment I got in until the moment I got out. It was a long monologue about the criminal rich and I was too frightened to tell him I owned a car.

Fifty-six

The headache was killing me, though I rarely have headaches. In fact until I was 30 I used to boast and repeat to all those around me that I had never had a headache. Those days are past and here I was standing in Mohamed Farid Street downtown with an agonising headache.

A taxi approached me and slowed down without stopping, so I had to shout out: "Agouza...Agouza." The driver stopped 30 yards beyond me and I ran to catch him in case he changed his mind and left me, which often happens for metaphysical reasons incomprehensible to poor people like me. I trod in a pool of sewage water which I had not noticed and which extended from under the car stopped on the side of the street.

It is something to have found a taxi but it was out of the frying pan into the fire. I found the driver was a young man of no more than 25 and he had turned up the volume on the cassette player to levels beyond international standards for the headache which was killing me.

When I asked him, with ample politeness, to turn down the volume, I suddenly found him deep in a conversation at a stage we should not have reached for at least another five minutes. "You mean, if that was the Koran, could you have told me to turn down the volume?" he shouted.

At first I didn't understand the connection between my request and what he had said, then it dawned on me that he was listing to a sermon and then I noticed a large number of pictures of Pope Cyril and Pope Shenouda surrounding me on every side, to show everyone that he was Christian. I cannot deny that I was surprised at the driver's behaviour, since Egypt's Christians don't generally rush into confrontations of this kind and since none of the Christian friends I know make much show of performing their religious duties. I never heard any of them say: 'I'm going to church today', unlike my Muslim friends, who never tire of announcing that they performed their prayers or fasted – 'I performed the afternoon prayer' or 'Because I didn't have time to perform the afternoon prayer' or 'I'm really tired because I'm fasting today.'

I've never understood the reason for that. Does it have something to do with the nature of each religion? Or is it because Christians are a minority in Egypt, or maybe I don't know because the headache has a hold on my head like a thug holding the shirt of the man he's beating.

I thought of withdrawing from the conversation but I decided to respond:

"Yes, I would tell you to turn it down," I said. "And for your information, as soon as I get in a taxi and find the driver playing the Koran and chatting with me, I quote the Koran at him: 'And when the Koran is recited, then listen to it and remain silent, that mercy may be shown to you.' (The Elevated Places, v.204), and I ask him to turn the tape off."

The driver grew more irritated, as if he hadn't heard what I said. "I won't turn it down and if you don't like it you can get out," he said.

Now I pretended to be irritated. "For a start, how do you know I'm Muslim? Is it written on my forehead? Couldn't I be a Christian with a headache, or must I hang a cross around my neck, or do I need to have hardened skin on my forehead from praying all the time, so you can classify your passengers?" I said.

"Look, this is my taxi," the driver said. "I won't turn it down. I want to listen. Are you going to get out or shall I carry on?"

I held my tongue and he drove on. I thought of talking to him about the principle of moderation in the exercise of one's rights and that his right must end where the rights of others start. But then I remembered that what I was thinking was meaningless nonsense in the streets of Egypt, which ring with shouts of every kind, where loudspeakers surround us and no one can open his mouth.

One side of the tape had ended and the driver quickly put the other side on. Silence reigned for some moments as we waited at the traffic lights near the High Court building. I noticed that the tensed muscles of his face began to relax a little. I was sitting on the back seat and I began to examine him. He was younger than I expected, perhaps 20 years old, and it looked like his hair had not seen a comb for ages. From the way he spoke he did not appear to have much education. Probably it had stopped after primary school.

I took out a piece of chocolate and offered it to him in the hope that it would relieve a little of the tension. When he turned it down, I said: "It's better than smoking cigarettes. Go on then, smoke."

He took the chocolate reluctantly.

"Why are you so fanatical?" I asked him.

"What makes you think I'm a fanatic?" he answered.

"Go on, tell me what the matter is."

We were close to the incline up to the Sixth of October Bridge and at the start of the ramp a crowd of people came forward to shout out their destinations in the hope that the driver would stop for them. He turned off the tape to hear their shouts – Embaba, el-Warrak, Boulak el-Dakrour. He didn't stop but drove up the ramp. The bridge was jam-packed and after a long silence, he sighed and started to speak:

"My brother spoke to me just now. He's the only success

in our family. That brother's a genius, a lecturer in the sociology department of the Faculty of Humanities."

"That's good," I said.

"Today the professor who's supervising his thesis postponed the examination yet again. The son of a bitch has been stringing him along for several years. Frankly he's persecuting him because he's Christian. In the Faculty of Literature they gang up to obstruct anyone who's Christian."

Any objection from me would have unleashed an enormous outburst of anger inside him and, besides, what he said might be true. I had witnessed and known about such cases before. I didn't know exactly what I should say so I decided to keep quiet, silent like all the silent people in society around me.

Fifty-seven

"I've been thinking about this day for four months. I sat down every day and said: 'Fifty days to go' or 'Forty-five days to go.' It's been a nightmare haunting me. It's been like a curse hanging over me and from which I could not escape. You see, renewing one's driving licence is something that comes around every three years and every time you obliterate the memory of what happens in those few days. The three years pass in a flash and you find you don't know what to do.

"Anyway, I'll tell you the story of this exhausting task and by the time we reach Shubra I'll have finished the story for you and we'll fill the time.

"I went to the Cairo Traffic Department in Salam City, and I live in Dar el-Salam, That makes two Salams, but to get from my place to the traffic department I have to take three buses, with a fight for each one, in other words it takes me at least two hours. I reached the Traffic Department and found out what was needed – a police document with my finger-prints and a photograph, social insurance, a certificate from the union, payment receipts, in other words, and a medical examination certificate.

"Of course to get from the traffic department to the

insurance place, Basatin branch, which is in Maadi, would take three hours, because that's in the far north of the city and the other's in the far south, so I would have arrived after they closed.

"The next day I went to the insurance office and went in to see the official who assesses the insurance, and he said: 'Go and pay and then come back to me.' So I went to the cashier's office and the queue was unbelievable. I paid about 424 pounds for the three years and went back to the first guy. He made out the receipt for me and told me to go upstairs to sign and get a stamp and then come back to him. I went upstairs and went in to see the woman there. 'Please I want to sign and get a stamp,' I said. She told me to go see Mrs So-and-so. Mrs So-and-so sent me to Mrs Such-and-such. I did a complete circle. Anyway, I signed and she told me to go to the manager woman's office for her to stamp my papers in the other room. I went in and the manager was in the bathroom. Would she come out and show her face? No way. I thought she must be giving birth. Anyway after about an hour she did show up and stamped the papers. All well and good. I went downstairs to the first clerk and sat waiting about half an hour. He had a look at the paper and said: 'That's fine, off you go.' Okay, but couldn't I have left right from the start, without hanging around to see him? Anyway I was out.

"Of course it wouldn't have done to do the union bit the same day because they are naturally in two different directions, because the union's in Abdou Pasha in Abbasia, and getting from Maadi to Abbasia is another story.

"The next day I went to the union in Abdou Pasha and said: 'Good morning, good morning.' I gave him the old union cards and he asked for 105 pounds. 'Why 105 for God's sake?' I asked him. 'It's gone up, didn't you know?' he said. 'No, really, no one told me. They hide these things from me because I have a bad heart, even before I came here,' I said. 'Anyway, it's hanging on the wall there, go and see for yourself,' he said. 'Okay,' I said. I went to see the piece of paper on the wall and added up the fees and found the total came to 83 pounds. I went back to him and said: 'Look, it's 83 pounds, so how come you're saying it's 105?' 'It's being implemented retroactively and you have to pay the increase of the last three years.' 'And the three years I paid for three years ago?' I said. He shook his head. 'There's something called retroactive effect?' I said. 'You should have passed a law to bring it in at the time.' He waved his hand. 'That's the system,' he said. 'Are you going to pay or aren't you?'

"I didn't have a choice so of course I'd pay. I paid but there was a question bugging me. 'Can I ask you a question, just out of interest?' 'Go ahead.' 'What do we benefit from all this money we pay?' 'Nothing.' He said. 'You say it straight to my face, in all simplicity, thank you.'

"Anyway, what caught my attention was another guy who was paying his union fees and was asking why this and why that. They told him it's a friendship fund. He told them: 'I just want to pay the union, I don't need anyone to come to my funeral when I die. That's none of your business. I don't want to pay for the friendship fund.' Anyway when I left the argument was still raging and I don't know what happened with the guy.

"I haven't put you to sleep, I hope. No. You still look awake so I'll carry on. The next day I went up to the police document place where I live in the Basatin police station. Anyway I went to the station, and it was a run around and torture. Why? I'll tell you.

"After I'd stood in a long queue the policeman told me to go get a police stamp. I went in to get the police stamp and they told me: 'No, go to the police station in Maadi or Khalifa.' 'Why there?' I said, 'The stamps there look nicer?' 'No, funny guy,' they said, 'There they have police stamps and here we don't.' 'What do you mean? Isn't this a police station as well so how come you don't have any?' 'Please, don't hold us up. Get out of the way. Next, please.'

"Anyway I took a taxi back and forth to Maadi police station and paid 12 pounds to get a three-pound police stamp. Then I went back to stand at the back of the queue. It was real torture. Anyway that was Thursday and they told me I could pick up the police document on Saturday. I went early on Saturday to take it straight away. Of course I was dreaming. I waited outside and the pashas were having beans for breakfast. The paper still hadn't turned up. Anyway in the end I got the document but I couldn't get to the traffic department the same day. Disaster, because the owner of the taxi was going to get another driver to replace me.

"The next day I went to the traffic department, from Dar el-Salam to Salam City, toughened from all the battles I had been through and with the papers in my pocket. They told me: 'The medical department.' I went out to the medical department and found people standing selling medical certificates. 'Yes, yes, anyone want certificates, anyone want certificates?' one guy was shouting. Like peddlars, I mean. Anyway, I got a form from him and asked him how much it was. He said two pounds. A guy who by chance was passing by in the street told me: 'Hey man, they'll give you those for free upstairs. The peddlars gave a dirty look to the man who told me. The man who sold me the paper came up and he didn't want to make a scene. 'If my paper doesn't work, bring it back and I'll give you the money,' he said.

"I went upstairs to the window and the man took the photograph off the piece of paper I had bought for two pounds. I asked him: 'Don't you want that paper?' He said no, so I said: 'Well, give it to me.' I took it and went downstairs to the man who was selling them and said: 'Up to your word?' He said okay and I got two pounds from him.

"Anyway we fixed a time for the medical. I'd made it for Saturday but they said: 'Come on Tuesday.' I thought I'd grab the chance and while I was at it do the traffic violations document. Outside I found every layabout in town.

"'Sir, sir, can we do the violations certificate for you?' 'How much will it cost?' I asked. 'Ten pounds, five pounds which the guy inside takes and five pounds towards our livelihood.' 'What do you mean, livelihood?' 'As sustenance from God, and for our trouble and effort,' he said. 'Well, if you find a livelihood lying around then give me a call. We all need a livelihood,' I said. 'You'll stand in the line and go through hell and you wouldn't be able to finish your business with the people inside,' he said. 'I don't have anything else to do,' I said, 'the day's completely ruined and I'm waiting for the medical.'

"I left him and stood in the queue. Of course we waited ages. I bought the form for five pounds and handed it in to the traffic department. He took another five pounds, although I didn't have any traffic offences. But they have to take money. They call it winter relief or summer relief or anything. I waited about two hours and of course there was no shade or anything and we were scorched by the sun until we couldn't take any more. Then they called us on the loudspeaker and I got my certificate and off I went. It was a tough day.

"Fallen asleep? All that was just talk, but if you'd been with me what would have happened? Okay, I'll carry on, though it's clear you'd rather sleep than hear my voice.

"I waited till Tuesday and I don't want to tell you how crowded it was. There were queues around the block. I waited in a queue as long as a snake and the man was standing there shouting out all the time: 'Come on, everyone get ready and tell us good morning.' Of course, this 'good morning' meant everyone should give him a tip. I paid a pound and I went in, thank God, and did the form and then we went into the doctor to have our nerves and our eyes checked. A very strange thing happened to do with glasses. The driver right in front of me was renewing his licence and it had expired about six years ago. He kept saying he wanted to take the test with his glasses on but the doctor refused. She said: 'No, see what the traffic department says first. It's been six years since you renewed the licence and your photo on the licence is without glasses. The man said: 'How am I going to earn a living?' Anyway she told him to take the test without glasses and he said he wouldn't see anything. She said: 'Really, go and ask at the traffic department.' The man went out screaming. I went in after him and I had butterflies in my stomach. I was holding the glasses in my hand and my hand was shaking. I'd just had them made about a week ago for the test. I said to her: 'In the photo I'm not wearing glasses.' She said: 'Never mind, come and put on your glasses, no problem.' Then in a loud voice she said: 'See how we don't want to make life complicated for you. Here's an old guy whose licence hasn't expired and he's renewing it, no problem, and I'll write on the test: 'Without glasses.'

"Of course my case was exactly the same as that of the guy before me, but you never can tell. Anyway I did the test with glasses on and it went just fine. All this business took three hours non-stop in the crowd and they told me to come to the traffic department in two days' time.

"I went on Thursday and the sun was fierce. I said: 'That's nice. My bald spot'll get roasted. I stood in the line from one end to the other and then the woman said: 'Go and pay the fee at the cash desk for the computer picture.' The computer turned out to be out of order, but I paid for the computer picture anyway and I went back to the back of the line again and when I got to the front she said we needed some tax stamps. So I left the line and went to get some tax stamps, and then I went to the back of the line again. For all that time there was no shade from the sun or anything and by the end of it you could have fried an egg on my bald spot. Anyway, I handed the papers to the woman at the desk. She looked at them and said: 'You're done, sir, everything's in order, wait till you hear your name to get your licence, but the computer's down so you'll only get a temporary slip of paper.' I said: 'Madam, give me anything, even if it's written on toilet paper. What matters is that we can drive down the street with it and if anyone stops us we can produce it.' I took myself off and waited close to two hours for someone to call my name. Nothing, and it was close to two o'clock and the civil servants were about to start leaving.

"There were two of us left who hadn't been called. The other guy was called Nader, a rather fat and friendly driver. We went to ask at the window and we surprised to hear that they couldn't find our files. Nader slipped some money into her hand and said: 'Try and make us a new file or anything. Do what you can.' She put the money in her bag and made two files and said: 'That's a permit for three months. If we can't find your file, you'll have to bring copies of your certificates, birth certificates and all that. I took the three-month permit and recited the Elephant chapter of the Koran. I couldn't believe it.

"When I'm lying in bed I like to daydream: Will they find the file? Will the computer be repaired? It's a nightmare that won't end. Have any idea why they do this to us?"

Fifty-eight

Ramadan, just before the cannon was fired to mark the end of the fast, and I was carrying a big picture, waiting for a taxi to appear, if necessary from the sky. It was about 10 minutes before the cannon and it's hard to find a taxi at that time. But divine intervention sent one to me like an angel on the night of Revelation. He truly was a black angel with black wings coming from the black south, the most beautiful part of Egypt, Aswan, with a heart that was black, the colour of purity and beauty.

"The picture's very big," said the driver. "It won't fit on the back seat. Would you like me to tie it to the roof rack?"

"We don't have time for that if we're to be in time for the *iftar* meal," I said.

"Nothing will happen if we're a few minutes late," he said.

The black angel got out of the taxi and fixed the picture to the roof of the car and off we went, gently and without hurry. The man was in his late 50s, with gentle features and a melodious voice.

"Are you an artist?" he asked.

"No, but I was just visiting an artist friend of mine," I said.

"Portrait or landscape?"

"I really don't know exactly. That's a very specialist question. Are you an artist?" I said.

"I used to like painting a lot. Ah yes, I used to paint."

"Used to. And why did you stop?" I asked him.

"Ah, I've stopped lots of things. As you go along you leave things behind you and it's impossible to go back to them. The hands of the clock only move forward."

"So you gave up painting, and then?" I asked.

"Life's journey is long as you make your way along it. I've been around, traveled far and wide, been to Spain, Italy and France. I stayed in France a while and worked as a messenger in an Egyptian office. There on Sunday I used to go to the Louvre, because on Sundays it's free. Culture for everyone. I used to sit all day long enjoying myself. I really loved David's painting of the consecration of Napoleon. It has extraordinary detail and beautiful lighting effects. It's a big painting, about ten metres by six and he painted it in 1805. But as you can see I'm done roving and here I am taking you to your destination."

"If you like painting that much, you should paint," I said.

"I like very many things. I waste all my money on my hobbies. I work on the taxi for a few hours then I stay at home the rest of the day and don't move. It's the nest where I get away from the world. It try to make it a comfortable nest. I live on the ground floor in Kattamia and I have a garden in front of the house. That garden I consider my own, and I work in it every day. I've planted honeysuckle, hyacinth beans, dieffenbachia and bougainvillea. I've also planted hibiscus with red flowers. That closes by day and opens at night. I'm also fond of birds. I have a big cage with about 20 birds in it. My wife just had a big argument with me yesterday because I bought a pair of birds for 250 pounds. Those are birds that come from Brazil, really beautiful and gentle, but they won't breed in Egypt.

"How, oh how, could I spend all that money on a pair of birds?

"I also have fish tanks with fantails and guppies.

"And I've made an Arabian-style sitting area on the ground, surrounded by the fish tanks and the birds, and in front of me through the window there's the garden. I feel like I'm in paradise far from the hell of Cairo."

"That sounds really beautiful," I said.

"Thanks. You know, sir, when I'm at home I feel outside place and outside time. I watch the fish and listen to the chirping of the birds and at night I can smell the honeysuckle. You should pay me a visit some time."

He talked to me about plants, art, fish, birds and beauty and he was an encyclopaedia on every subject. Where did he get all this knowledge? He complained to me of his son, that he wanted to obtain everything without any effort. He complained of his ignorance and remembered how he and his colleagues would go every evening for extra lessons in some field or other. He complained to me of how the world had made his son like this.

In the end that black angel left the taste of sugar in my mouth and the scent of honeysuckle in my soul. He made me, for the first time in ages, have my breakfast slowly, without haste, contemplating everything around me.

In the end he made me try to make my house a nest like the one he had described. But where can I find wings like his?

Glossary of words, names and events

1973 Arab-Israeli war – known in the Arab world as the Ramadan War and in Israel as the Yom Kippur War. It began on October 6 1973 when Egypt and Syria began an offensive to regain their territories (the Sinai peninsula and Golan Heights, respectively) which had been occupied by Israel in 1967. Fighting ended on October 24 with a UN-imposed ceasefire.

Adel Imam – Egyptian actor.

Ahmed Nazif – prime minister of Egypt. He has held office since 2004. His name means 'Mr Clean' in Arabic.

Ahmed Zeweil – awarded the Nobel prize in 1999 for his work on the changes in atoms during chemical reactions.

Camp David – referring to the peace deal signed between Egypt and Israel in 1979. The hatred felt in the Arab world against Egyptian President Anwar Sadat for negotiating with Israel led to his assassination two years later.

Faragallah – type of mincemeat named for the company that produces it.

hijab – a woman's head covering.

Heneidi – Mohamed Heneidi is a comedy actor who first became popular about 10 years ago.

inshallah – literally 'God willing'.

Jihan el-Sadat – wife of former president Anwar Sadat. She has devoted herself to public service and the advancement of women's rights.

Kefaya movement – 'kefaya' means 'enough' in Arabic and is the unofficial name of the Egyptian Movement for Change, a grassroots coalition that draws its support from across Egypt's political spectrum to oppose President Hosni Mubarak's presidency.

Khan el-Khalili – a market in the old city of Cairo and the site of a suicide attack in April 2005 which killed 21 people.

Koshari – An Egyptian 'fast-food' made with lentils and chilli.

Mahmoud Mukhtar – Considered the father of modern Egyptian sculpture. He died aged 43 in 1934.

Mohamed Saad – actor who has been active since 2000. El Lembi was one of his first films and the comedy became one of the highest-grossing films in Egyptian cinema.

Mubarak – Mohammed Hosni Mubarak became president of Egypt after the assassination of Sadat in 1981.

Muslim Brotherhood – the largest political opposition movement in many Arab nations, particularly Egypt. Established in 1928 in Egypt, it has been outlawed since the mid 1950s. Nevertheless, in Egypt's 2005 elections the Brotherhood's candidates, who must run as independents due to their illegal status as a political party, won 20 per cent of all seats to form the largest opposition bloc.

Nasser – Abdul Nasser. One of the leaders of the revolution that ousted the king in 1952. He became president in 1954.

Pasha – an honorific, equivalent to 'Sir'.

piastres – unit of currency with 100 piastres making one Egyptian pound. The exchange rate for 2007 was approximately 5.5 Egyptian pounds per one US dollar.

Sadat – Anwar Sadat. President of Egypt from 1970 to 1981. He was assassinated during a military parade.

Safaga – port on the Red Sea to which the *al-Salam Boccaccio* was sailing from Saudi Arabia in February 2006 when it sank. More than 1,000 died in the tragedy.

Sharon – Ariel Sharon, former prime minister of Israel, suffered a severe stroke in December 2006. A year later he was still in a deep coma.

Sultan Qaboos – Ruler of the kingdom of Oman.

Toshka – a huge engineering project inaugurated by President Hosni Mubarak in 1997 which pumps water from the Nile into natural depressions adjacent to the river in south-west Egypt. The Toshka project covers thousands of square kilometres and is considered a modern engineering feat.

Umm Kalsoum – Egyptian singer (1898-1975). She is still recognised as the Arab world's most famous and distinguished singer of the 20th century.

Yehia al-Fakharani – famous Egyptian actor.